A

A ghost mystery set in Lincolnshire, England, United Kingdom.

The first of the
James Hansone Ghost Mysteries

By Paul Money

A Ghostly Diversion

Copyright Notice

Astrospace Publications
18 College Park, Horncastle, Lincolnshire LN9 6RE
www.astrospace.co.uk

Copyright © Paul Money February 2016 / POD October 2020 / update August 2022
All rights reserved.

The right of Paul Money to be identified as the author of this work has been asserted by him in accordance with the Copyright, Designs and Patents Act 1988.

All the characters in the story are fictional and any resemblance to real persons either living or dead is purely coincidental.
No part of this book may be reproduced in any form other than that which it was purchased and without the written permission of the author.
This book is licensed for your personal enjoyment only.
This book may not be re-sold or given away to other people in
either this or any other format.

Language: UK English

Cover:
Principal designer: Cupit/Rebecca Turner
Based on original ideas by Paul Money

Cover photos:
Cover photos: Fotolia.com
© Sean Gladwell © vladimirfloyd © carljl

Acknowledgements

The author would like to acknowledge the support and help of his wife, Lorraine, in listening to the idea of the story, how it developed and giving both invaluable advice and editing ideas as the story progressed. He would also like to thank the following for their advice, informed wisdom, patience, and encouragement as this book progressed from a few pages to a full-blown novel:

Gill Hart
Mark Lenton
Pat & Keith Money (Mum & Dad)
Margaret Slater (Mum 2 aka Mum in Law)
Jane Annetts
Sally Wood
Rebecca Turner

Thanks also go to:
Catherine Ryan Howard, who's e book about self-publishing helped get 'A Ghostly Diversion' into shape and gave invaluable advice on self-publishing.
and
Notjohn's Guides to Publishing 2016

Finally, grateful thanks for the wonderful help and support of Cupit Print of Horncastle for their work on the original print edition and cover for both the printed edition, the Kindle and the POD edition.

A Ghostly Diversion

Preface

An ongoing set of roadworks.
A dark blue Mercedes.
A diversion.
A derelict cottage.
A young girls face at a broken window.
A fifty-year-old mystery.

James Hansone faces all the above and much more, all because of a diversion to avoid roadworks one morning. A relative newcomer to the rural county of Lincolnshire, he likes his job, his new home and loves his wife, Helen.

He is also a sceptic of all things paranormal.

Until the day of the diversion...

'Wolds View' cottage holds a mystery about a young girl who disappeared fifty years earlier. A missing person's case that's stalled and long forgotten.

As strange sightings begin to occur to him, James Hansone finds himself increasingly drawn into trying to discover:

who she is

whether he can find out who or what caused her death

and why he seems to be the only one that can see her...

A Ghostly Diversion

Prologue

Limbo.

A world between worlds. Neither here nor beyond.
Unable to go back, unable to pass on.
A restless state for anyone there.

It takes her several weeks before she can achieve form, but she realises she is now a lost soul.

Understanding begins to dawn as to why she remains stuck between states.
No one knows where she lies.
No one can give her justice.
No one can bring her peace.

Destined to forever roam old ground and not new.

Desperately, she finds her way home, but her beloved father and mother can't see her. She reaches out to them but has no touch and so she drifts aimlessly, wandering the places of her old life searching for an answer.

Lost.

More solitary weeks pass.

One evening her mother retires to bed as her father sits in the living room whilst a single lamp gently illuminates the scene. Half asleep, a glass of whiskey in his hand, a half empty bottle on the small table beside him.
She hesitantly drifts forward knowing he can't see his 'little poppet'.

A Ghostly Diversion

She's wrong.
He looks up.
Eyes brighten, then stare in horror as comprehension dawns and his worst fear is realised.

She is never coming back.

She backs away and fades from view as he reaches out to her, tears in his eyes wishing it wasn't true.
Muscles tighten.
Muscles seize.
An uncertain smile is frozen on his face as he realises at that instant what it means, but that also he can at last be at peace knowing the truth.
He slumps forward and the glass drops to the floor with a crash. Her mother rushes down and is inconsolable at what she finds.

The girl flees the house distraught at what she might have caused.

A couple of weeks pass.

The funeral allows him to leave this world, to pass beyond, to be at peace.
But she remains trapped in limbo.

Trapped between worlds and unable to pass on to be with her beloved father.

Neither here nor beyond.
Unable to go back.
Unable to pass on.
Trapped with no hope of being found.

A Ghostly Diversion

No hope of attaining peace.
No hope of resolution.
No hope of justice.
No hope.
No hope…

Until many years later…

A Ghostly Diversion

1: A Ray of Hope…

The wet slate grey road curved round into the distance, disappearing off to the right behind a line of trees. Meanwhile the queue of cars, vans and lorries followed like lost sheep.

Start, stop.
And again.
Start, stop.
Start.
Ahh a little further this time, then …
Stop.
Bugger!

James Hansone cocked his head to one side and drummed the fingers of his right hand against the dashboard for the umpteenth time, feeling the frustration grow. He had himself to blame, for the estimated two-month long roadworks had been announced several weeks earlier, but he, like a lot of drivers apparently, had taken the chance that there would be a good flow to the traffic control.

Ha! Fat chance!

He drummed his fingers again, this time to an almost long forgotten tune that somehow had drifted into his consciousness. Something to do with polka dots and bikinis but the title just wouldn't come to him. He shook his head and then, as if on cue, the traffic rolled a few car lengths further on.

He looked at his watch; 8:40 a.m. Twenty minutes to do almost, he did a quick mental calculation, eighteen more miles in order to get to work. Not possible now without breaking the speed limit and, with the queue, pretty much no chance of that happening if he was honest with himself. Well, he had a semi reasonable excuse as the traffic chaos had already been mentioned on the radio so he could use that this time if his boss complained.

And start earlier tomorrow, he thought.

The traffic all rolled on again for a few more metres as the lights seemed to briefly change to green then almost as quickly turn back to red. There just *had* to be a fault with it.

It looked hopeless.

"Bet it'll be 9:15 or so at the very least, before I get to work", he said to himself. 'Wait until tonight', he wondered, as his mind drifted to Helen, his wife. She'll remind him that she had warned to start off earlier, but no, he was stubborn and didn't like the thought of getting up any earlier, he liked his bed!

He smiled as he thought of Helen.

They had been happily married for nearly twenty years and had begun to think about a big change such as moving to another area. However, the company James worked for had made the decision for them by deciding to relocate to Lincolnshire from the phenomenally expensive outskirts of London. So, the move was actually down to the fact that the firm he worked for had decided to close the office in London and relocate to the much cheaper county of Lincolnshire. If he wanted to keep his job then James, and Helen, had little option but to move from their home in Albury.

On investigation, the rural market town of Horncastle had proved ideal, if a little quaint with its many antiques centres. The firm didn't mind the, normally, twenty-five-minute drive into the new premises on a relatively new industrial estate on the outskirts of Lincoln. It was a long cry from the fifty-minute commute on the train James was used to, so at least that was a blessing. Lincolnshire still retained wide open spaces and their new home was bigger and had large gardens at front and rear – something which they had longed for whilst being 'down south'. In the end their fears about moving had been unfounded and James and Helen had settled in well.

But now the main road to Lincoln was being dug up and resurfaced – apparently for the third time in as many years and the locals had started to call the stretch of the A158 he was stuck on, '*the trench*'!

James grimaced as he looked again at his watch and added another five minutes to his estimated arrival time at work. Up ahead lay a small village with several sharp bends, he couldn't quite see the village sign for it. One day, he promised himself, he would remember its name. For now, it was just beyond the village that the longest section of the roadworks was taking place. It had to be done of course but it always seemed to be at the wrong time for everyone and *sooo* inconvenient.

Bored, he looked for amusement at the various vehicle colours ahead of him in the queue. Silver, silver, silver, silver again (why is silver the main colour nowadays? Boring or what!), deep metallic blue, white van man (he grinned to himself), silver, white, blue van (surprise), lorry, green (yuk!). Oh surprise, a tractor too with a long trailer behind it.

He shook his head.

Fed up even more so now, he sighed again and looked around at the rolling countryside. Lovely, he thought, gazing at their adopted county. Over in the distance lay several clumps of woodland, some of which was of a pine like nature, probably one of the many Forestry Commission managed areas in the county, he figured. He knew that somewhere over in that direction there was an actual forest trail open to the public and he resolved to take Helen there and explore it.

Noting that it seemed to take almost five full minutes for the lights to change, he leaned over and fished his small pair of binoculars out of the glove compartment. Since moving up into the countryside he'd bought a pair as there was so much to the wide-open scenery to explore.

He'd made a point of keeping the binoculars in the car just in case he spotted something interesting like a buzzard. He'd seen one a few weeks back along with a Kestrel a little later and regretted not having anything to view them with. He scanned the distant rolling countryside, spying Lincoln Cathedral some twenty or so miles in the distance as the crow flies, then moved round to his right until suddenly the cars up ahead were in the way.

The white car had Irish plates and what appeared to be two young women were having an animated discussion, perhaps they were late for something too, he wondered. Perhaps they were heading for East Midlands Airport and were already panicking about missing the flight.

He shrugged to himself and hoped they wouldn't miss it if that was the case.

Turning back to his left there lay an area of deciduous woods rich in ash and sycamore in the distance, perhaps part of a private farm or estate. They were lucky to have retained their ash trees, James thought, especially after the widespread disease that had wiped out so many of the ash trees in the UK and Europe.

He was jolted out of his wanderings and back to reality as the traffic began to move again. Slowly they moved forward and now he was on the outskirts of the village known as Baumber as the sign ahead announced the village to the world and their cars. 'Must really make the effort to remember that', he thought, and just as quickly mentally added he probably wouldn't be able to forget it after the delays due to the roadworks.

Just a little further along the main road lay a turning on the left for a small side road. He eyed it and began weighing up options. Of course, long ago without a proper map of the area he would have had no idea where he could end up. Not so now, with sat navs and smart phone apps, he could just punch the details in and call up the area on the screen display. He glanced down at his smart phone located in its slot on the dashboard and noted the almost non-existent signal.

Typical! In London and Albury, he'd never had poor service but here it seemed his chosen network was a hit and miss affair. Perhaps he needed to change his service provider… He dismissed the idea for the moment, pit down the binoculars on the passenger seat and went back to watching the traffic as it began to move again.

Start.

Five car lengths this time before once again…

A Ghostly Diversion

Stop.

He felt his frustration build a little more. What on Earth were they doing further up that could make it this bad, he wondered. He patiently waited. Then, as the lights changed to green again, the dark metallic blue Mercedes, two cars ahead, caught his eye as it had reached the turning and suddenly indicated. It swung left and speeded up as it drove down the lane disappearing out of sight behind some buildings. The cars ahead moved forward and quickly filled the gap left by the Mercedes. Just then, the lights also changed again, all of a sudden, James reached it and turned left on a whim.

Why?

He didn't know.

It just seemed a good idea.

Spur of the moment kind of thing.

Even as his car sped down the lane the doubts began swirling in his mind. Looking at the farm buildings whizzing by he couldn't help thinking, 'what was he doing?' The sign he'd only just glimpsed said somewhere called Grasceby. He had no idea where Grasceby was, whether he could get back to the main road after it, whether it would bring him out after the roadworks or, worse still, bring him right out in the middle of the roadworks again. That last would be his typical run of luck!

Perhaps time to use the in-car systems now - but his curiosity was piqued, and he felt a thrill he hadn't experienced for a long time.

It felt like a boy's adventure and a surge of excitement passed through him!

The Mercedes ahead was clearly breaking the speed limit and disappeared round a slight bend only to reappear a little further on where the trees parted to give a clear view of the road.

"What's done is done" James muttered out loud as he made up his mind and continued along this diversion. Down a slight slope then up past the clearing where he'd spotted the Mercedes just a few moments earlier. He continued onwards and he realised he was enjoying this new challenge with its thrill of the unknown.

At least he was moving!

He liked that.

A lot.

Even on the balance of it he didn't quite know where it would lead him to but for a few short moments he didn't seem to care. Up ahead the road veered sharply to the left and, at first, James couldn't see anything of the Merc. But then, in the corner of his right eye, a glint of light in the shade of metallic blue caught his attention. As he approached the sharp bend, he realised there was a turning to the right and that was where the Merc had gone.

The other driver certainly seemed to know what he was doing so, with a shrug, James also took the same turning. Baumber lay ahead – "BAUMBER!" He called out loud to no one as he realised that was where he'd just come from! Grasceby, the village the earlier signpost had mentioned didn't lie ahead. Without realising it he'd overshot a well concealed side lane off to the left and an almost hidden and partially damaged signpost pointed off that way to it.

He pulled over onto the grass verge and let his annoyance with himself calm down. It was bad enough the fact that the Merc had now vanished

A Ghostly Diversion

from sight so he could no longer follow it. But now he was beginning to feel slightly foolish for driving off on what may well turn out to be a wild goose chase on a road or roads he didn't know. What's more, it could make him even later for work and, although he had a good working relationship with his boss, Mark, there was after all a limit to what you could get away with when it came to excuses.

James looked back at the almost obscured signpost and then down at the display console of the car. He sighed and, bringing up the mapping app, decided it was time to find out where Grasceby was in relation to where he was going. The screen sprung to life, and he scanned the map detail presented to him. Would you credit it, but Grasceby was shown with a very small road twisting and turning from Baumber with a couple of other turnoffs to another small village as well to the north. Best of all by following the road through Grasceby and on for a couple more miles past what looked to be a disused airfield, now marked as an industrial estate, the road joined a larger one. That in turn led back to the main road taking him to the market town of Wragby and then onto the main road towards Lincoln.

Not such a bad idea after all to take the diversion, he mused. Reversing the car, James turned onto the new lane and continued his journey, immediately meeting a car coming the other way. He just managed to steer onto the verge allowing the two cars to miss each other by inches and he tried to shrug an apology to the other. They were not impressed as indicated by the blaring of the other car's horn.

A Ghostly Diversion

"Sorry!" James said knowing full well they couldn't hear him but at least it made him feel better.

The road followed the gentle contours of the landscape as it turned and led into Grasceby, passing a sign to a nearby inn, too quickly to catch its name. Then he reached the small village itself. Mostly old cottages, but with a few newer developments and a couple of farms and a quite impressive looking church off to the left with what looked to be a rectory off to one side. James took note and, for a second or so, had a feeling that he'd been here before. But that was impossible as he and Helen had only moved up to Horncastle in the last couple of months and they'd not had much time to do any sightseeing yet.

Still that feeling of déjà vu came back several times as he drove round a small bend which followed a small trickle of a stream which, in turn, ended up in a quaint village pond. Set back behind a brick wall looked to be a large building that could easily be a modestly sized manor as the road snaked round to the left following the wall line that enclosed the manor.

'Very picturesque' he thought, as the road then curved to the right then back left and he again met another car coming the other way. A bit easier to avoid this time with no serious chance of collision. He breathed a sigh of relief and they passed each other safely.

"Missed me again" he stated out loud to no-one but himself. He continued past a farmyard noting that other drivers must have realised there was a diversion they could take to avoid the chaos on the main road.

A Ghostly Diversion

His mind wandered again. He was getting to like this part of Lincolnshire, with its rolling countryside, the wide fields, hedgerows, and isolated patches of woodland and small hamlets like Grasceby. Yes, they had done the right thing and he needed to make sure Helen and he did some exploring later in the summer.

The road veered to the left. Braking hard, he cursed his lapse of concentration, leaving a tyre mark in the soft verge side. Almost as if it was taunting him again the road turned sharply to the right taking it past a quite large expensive looking cottage and what seemed like stables. Far ahead about a mile or more the road stretched on a long straight and, just ahead he glimpsed a flash of metallic blue just disappearing round another bend way off in the distance.

James smiled at the brief view of the Merc and felt good with himself. At least he seemed to be on the right track and silently thanked the driver ahead for leading him this way. This straight part of the road was quite level with patchy hedgerows along the south side and woodland lining the right or north side stretching off into the distance with what looked like a kink in the tree line up ahead. He speeded up – not much chance of being caught out here he thought and, as he did so, he reached the apparent gap in the trees.

At that very same moment he felt as if an icy wind passed straight through his body as he shivered involuntarily and for a moment, he felt unwell. So much so he didn't notice the abandoned cottage on the right, situated slightly back and in the middle of the clearing of the wood. He quickly recovered and shook his head in bewilderment – well it was nearly summer, and it was a bright sunny morning in June, so the chill had taken him by surprise.

Cold?

Rubbish must have been his imagination he thought and slowed down to a more sensible speed. James checked the fan and the temperature controls wondering if the air conditioning had come on by accident, but everything seemed to be operating normally. He continued up the road, shook his head and settled back down to the journey. It didn't take long to navigate the roads that his mapping app was telling him to take. A winding section took him past a large, wooded area which opened out with a glimpse of the old airfield with a few abandoned rundown buildings running along its border and the hedge lined road he was on. Finally, after a couple more miles and another small junction he found himself at Wragby and was able to turn back towards his original route and destination. The cold sensation was quickly forgotten as he began to think up excuses for his boss for when he finally arrived at work.

It was going to be a long day!

#

Meanwhile, back at the cottage, a sad and lost soul stirred with an unexpected ray of new hope. She drifted to her favourite window to see what had roused her from a long quiescent state, but there was nothing there and her 'feeling' faded away again as quickly as it had begun. With

a sigh she turned back from the window and sat on her old bed to continue her long and lonely vigil.
　　　Lost and caught between worlds…

2: A trick of the light?

A few days later, James walked out of the front doors of the building towards the firm's staff car park with his boss and friend, Mark, who wore an annoyed frown on his face.

"So, we'll roll out the upgrade when we finally get the network components from Cambridge – or are we going to be waiting another few weeks whilst they get their act together?" James asked Mark as they approached their cars.

Mark in turn shrugged his shoulders.

"Yeah, that's the plan in theory. As soon as the components arrive, we'll get stuck into the upgrade. I knew we should have done it all ourselves, would have been quicker if you ask me. But no, the company wanted to use outside private contractors, and this is what we get in the end!"

They both walked on, the gravel of the car park crunching underfoot, James nodded his head thoughtfully. "Guess we'll know soon enough. Anyway, I'll think about our options just in case things do screw up. See you tomorrow."

Mark nodded and strolled off to his grey Audi, got in and in a flash was roaring out of the entrance. James smiled to himself; the boss was always quick off the mark when it came to home time.

James looked round and back at the building. It was on a new industrial estate just before you reached the city of Lincoln, the administrative capital of the county. Although quite modern looking on the outside, the practical needs of the high-tech firm that employed James and Mark had turned out to be spectacularly useless. Many of the specifications that the firm had been told would be installed before they moved up to this site had simply either been put in place in a rush or cheaper, poorer specification equipment had been installed, likely to save the company doing the work costs and make them a bit more profit.

The last couple of months had been very demanding as they had slowly found all the faults. They were trying to replace what equipment they could quickly in order to meet the demands of their clients. The computing and data analysis market was a cutthroat one and they couldn't afford to have the problems that had beset them since the move 'up north'. At one point the parent company had even contemplated abandoning the move entirely and going back to the old office, but they were already too far into the move with fifteen people relocated and not about to be moved again!

Mark was happy to some extent as he was originally from Lincolnshire, from Bardney, so he felt very much at home in this area and indeed had pushed for the move to Lincolnshire. James knew that Mark was now hoping he hadn't caused the firm problems now they'd had so much hassle since the move. However, he had settled back in very quickly once he'd found a property to his liking and, it had to be said, somewhat expensive taste and was determined to make the move work.

The original contractors that had done the re fitting would no doubt be hearing from the firm's solicitors shortly and rightly so, thought James.

A Ghostly Diversion

He sighed, turned back, unlocked his gold-coloured hatchback and got in. The roadworks were still on-going so that didn't help but there was always the shortcut he'd found the other day. 'Try it again tonight', he reflected. Earlier that morning had been annoying as he'd slipped up and kept to the main road – and been almost an hour late for work. "Won't do that again" he chuckled to himself as he recalled the look on Mark's face when he finally rolled in for work. He started the car and drove out the entrance onto the main road.

Down the road he remembered to take the turn off at Wragby and wound his way along the minor roads watching out for the small side lane signposted to – what was that village again – Graz - Grassby, GRASCEBY he suddenly saw on the sign just ahead and managed to slow down enough to turn into it safely. Coming from this direction there were initially more open fields with various patches of woodland up ahead on his left. Unfortunately, the hedge was a little overgrown and had obscured the side lane as it joined the road he was on.

A few isolated farms lay scattered around the area, but modern farming demanded larger fields. Over the years many of the original smaller farmsteads had simply been taken over by vast farming estates that now seemed to dominate the modern farming landscape. Ditches, drains and hedgerows had been torn up over the decades, but in more recent enlightened times some of them had been re-introduced when the effects on the landscape and wildlife had become better understood.

Even the disused airfield he had noted the other day had been torn up in places to give more

A Ghostly Diversion

land to growing crops. The rest had been turned into an industrial estate, but it looked like only one firm was located there. 'Another piece of our heritage slowly disappearing', he thought as he passed the dilapidated sign to the abandoned airfield.

One such drainage scheme was on the go along this new route as he now noticed an old drain was being renewed towards the north edge of the field system. It seemed oddly straight but then a lot of the fields around the area were nothing more than rectangles of land suited to machinery. The diggers were certainly making good progress he noted. He seemed to think there had to be two sets of workers as he was sure he'd seen another area of work closer to Grasceby when he'd come along this route from the other way just the other day.

Unfortunately, as the work continued so they were dragging some of the mud onto the road making James slow down a little and he noticed a sign warning of the mud on the road, 'too late' he thought as he'd already encountered the brown sludge splattered across the road.

The small, tarmacked road wound around the margins between two estates with sweeping views north towards the Lincolnshire Wolds on the left with the TV mast known as Belmont standing tall in the distance. On the right to the south, the Witham Valley lay partially hidden by the boundary of a nearby wood and the old airfield. Nearby was a popular local tourist attraction for walkers and nature lovers, the one James had spotted the other day with his binoculars whilst stuck in traffic.

The main woods lay on the right after a very steep left-hand bend with the dilapidated signpost indicating the site of RAF Grasceby he'd just passed. Part of the old concrete runway had been visible with large tufts of grass sticking up in patches where the concrete had crumbled, succumbing to the ravages of time. As he continued, the trees also began again on the left-hand side following the road like a ribbon of dark green with brown and grey bark mixed in.

Up ahead they seemed to dip back briefly on the left with what appeared to be a clearing, just after the main woods had come to an end on the right-hand side. The road itself stretched on for almost a mile in virtually a straight line. He subconsciously speeded up then checked himself and dropped back to the speed limit.

In the distance another car was heading towards him - quite fast really for the road, so James slowed down in anticipation. He was close to the clearing now and noticed some stonework and realised there was a cottage set back from the road and he drew onto the grass verge next to it to let the car past. The goose bumps caught him by surprise as the speeding car shot past with no hint of thanks for letting it pass and he shivered suddenly for no reason as a chill swept over his body.

He looked to the left at the cottage and for the first time noticed it was empty and abandoned with virtually all its windows smashed. The ground floor windows were boarded up, but it was clear the boarding's had fallen away from the upstairs windows.

Wild, out of control roses were trying to grow up the walls on the left-hand side; overall it was clear the cottage had not been lived in for quite a while. Still, he mused, the building did look in quite good shape and the main structure seemed to be straight and true. He briefly wondered how much it would fetch on the open market.

'Anyway, time to move on', he thought and as he turned away, he caught a glimpse of movement in the corner of his eye from the upstairs left-hand window. He stopped, blinked, and looked again but the empty window just stared back at him, and he nervously smiled to himself. He'd stopped the car on the verge as he looked at the cottage, now he quickly put it in gear and steered back onto the road.

'Strange that', he kept thinking – just for a moment he could have sworn there had been someone with long dark hair looking out the window. But that was silly, why would anyone be in a building like that? Abandoned, derelict, only a ghost would … he shivered again and became annoyed with himself for letting his imagination wander away like that.

No, ghosts were definitely nonsense, and he should know better than that. He was a confirmed sceptic of all things supernatural, although he had to admit he often liked watching films and TV series like that, mainly to pull them apart! He checked the road and pulled out slowly in case another speeding idiot should surprise him but this time it was all clear.

He picked up speed and drove away from the cottage refusing to look back again. The road rounded to the left into a tight bend and within a couple of miles James was passing through Grasceby, past its tall manor with its high wall surrounding it and he put the memory of the cottage and the fleeting glimpse of someone at the window to the back of his mind as he looked forward to getting home to Helen.

#

The spectre of the girl moved back to the window and watched him drive off into the distance. The strange feeling of hope she had again experienced lingered a little while as she felt his presence recede again. But once more sadness descended as she returned to her quiet vigil puzzled as to why she'd been affected so much by the passing stranger. Why now after all these years?

#

The next morning James deliberately set off for work early, much to Helen's surprise, and at Baumber he turned left onto the lane from the main road and drove along and passed through Grasceby. A strange feeling had stayed with him all night, but he didn't mention anything to Helen, it was too weird and slightly unnerving to him.

What would he say? 'Oh, by the way I may have seen a ghostly girl in an abandoned cottage on a back road to nowhere'. He ran those thoughts through his mind and shook his head. No way would he do that, only to look daft after all these years of being a hardened sceptic!

He rounded the last sharp bend and up ahead could just see the clearing, but from this viewpoint the cottage was set too far back to be easily noticed. He slowed the car as he approached.

Crawling almost to a standstill, he began scanning the cottage and especially the upper left

A Ghostly Diversion

room as he nervously half expected to see some zombie like creature leap out of the window and attack him, condemning him to a never-ending evil existence. He *would* be blessed (or was that cursed?) with a vivid imagination but on reflection watching the zombie apocalypse movie before going to bed last night perhaps had been a bad idea!

He hadn't noticed the Mercedes quickly catch up from behind him. The sharp blast on the car horn nearly sent James through the roof of the car in shock and certainly brought him back to his senses.

"Shit!"

He put his foot down and stalled the car, much to the annoyance of the other driver, who again gave a sharp double blast on the car horn. The man wound his window down and James heard a string of obscenities from the other driver, so he started the car up, pulled onto the side and apologetically waved the Merc past. It drove furiously off into the distance and was quickly lost to sight.

"Him again." James muttered as he recognised the car from the other day. He pulled back onto the road muttering curses at himself for being so foolish. "I imagined the damn thing" he said to himself, blaming the stress of his current workload and set off again, completely forgetting about the cottage.

For the rest of the week though, he couldn't bring himself to take the Grasceby route. Much to Helen's surprise and amusement, he found himself getting up early and heading off to work using the main road and putting up with the traffic chaos. A couple of weeks went by, and the derelict cottage became but a distant memory as things at work began to improve.

Finally, after much work and hassle the roadworks were at last finished and the main road became usable again, giving James no reason to ever go through the sleepy village of Grasceby or past the abandoned cottage again.

#

Back at the cottage the girl sighed as she silently continued her vigil, waiting for another chance to make herself seen to this intriguing person who had awakened her from years of sorrow. It seemed so unfair that after all these years for some unknown reason hope had been resurrected only to start to fade once again. She placed her head in her ghostly hands and silently sobbed as she remained sat on her old ghostly bed.

3: Diversion, take two...

"Now that was a well-earned break." Helen said and smiled at James as they unloaded the boot of the car with their suitcases and smaller luggage. Both were tanned and had clearly been abroad as witnessed by the tags on their luggage. OK so the UK summer was nearly over but who cares when you can jet off to sunny Florida for two weeks!

Kennedy Space Centre was clearly the favourite for James even though he wasn't particularly into space or the stars whilst the Everglades had been almost magical for Helen. They had both come back fully refreshed and raring to go, or so they thought. The excitement at seeing a rocket blast off from KSC was something neither of them would forget despite their normal lack of interest. Unfortunately, there had not been a manned flight scheduled for when they were there which was a bit of a disappointment. Instead, they'd got to see an orbiter mission to Jupiter lift off so at least that was something.

If they'd been able to take the holiday in November then there might have been the chance to see the historic first private mission to an asteroid, but Mark had been quite strict about when they could have their main holidays.

Back to the grindstone though as usual, but it didn't seem so bad now and news from the firm James worked for had been good just before they left for Florida, so things were looking up at last. A quick trip to the shops for much needed supplies and

A Ghostly Diversion

then they crashed out in bed as the jet lag finally hit them for six.

Still at least it was Monday the next day and, knowing they would arrive home very late on the Saturday night, James had booked the extra day off work as well, so when they finally crawled out of bed late in the morning they didn't care. Two weeks away and the garden was a mess! Lawns overgrown and the hedge – well it needed more than a simple trim, but they both got stuck in and by teatime things were at last beginning to look shipshape.

James walked over towards the shed and, hearing a car on the nearby road, looked up just in time to see the blue Mercedes drive by and race off down the road. "Bloody driver – thinks he owns the roads round here." He moaned out loud to nobody. Helen called over to him to see what he was talking about, and James waved to her that it was nothing. His thoughts turned briefly to the abandoned cottage but, shaking his head, he pushed it quickly out of mind and turned back to the garden wishing he hadn't seen the car.

#

The next day, work dragged slowly at first but gradually James got back into the swing of things. Mark was also more cheerful now their office computer systems were working properly, add to that a couple of new recruits had joined the firm as some people had left, missing their old homes and families down south.

So, Craig and Peter were welcomed into the fold after Mark had given them both a good

A Ghostly Diversion

sounding out for their suitability. James took an instant liking to Craig as he seemed a kindred spirit and didn't take things too seriously which couldn't be said of the staider, and oh so serious, Peter.

The day drew to a close and they all streamed out of the building ready for home time and James was quickly on the road. Very soon he was once again approaching Wragby but flashing blue lights up ahead meant trouble. A policewoman flagged him to stop, and he lowered the window to ask about the trouble.

"Serious incident sir, a petrol tanker has overturned at the marketplace junction, and we've had to close the whole road and evacuate the locals. Where are you heading to?" she asked.

"Horncastle." James replied and she paused and thought for just a brief moment.

"Best bet would be to go back until you see the turning for Goltho and Apley. Then head for Kingsthorpe and after that the signs for Bardney, easy enough to get to Horncastle from there sir from the signposts. Lucky you're in a car, larger vehicles are having to go back to the Lincoln bypass and take a much longer diversion." She smiled and he thanked her and turned the car around in the industrial estate entranceway that she'd indicated.

Bit of a long way round but not much choice he thought to himself and headed off back the way he'd come. The turning the officer had mentioned really struggled to be called a road with tufts of grass pushing up through the tarmac and dips in the surface enough to make you seasick! Now he could understand why the local news often carried reports and complaints about the state of the roads in the

A Ghostly Diversion

county. He found his way back onto the Bardney road and after a mile or so realised he knew this stretch.

Unfortunately.

A few more miles and his suspicions were confirmed when he once more saw the sign for Grasceby stating it was two and a half miles away. About to deliberately drive past it to avoid passing the cottage, James found himself compelled to turn into the lane and with a shrug he thought, 'what the heck'. He shouldn't go letting his imagination run riot, so he decided it was time to get it under control.

The wide-open fields beckoned once more and there, he noted, was the wood on the right and the disused airfield. Not far now, he nervously thought, then reigned in his mental wanderings before it began to make him start imagining all sorts of weird things. He drew closer to the cottage and instinctively slowed down. He again looked up at the upstairs windows and there framed in the left window the girl with the long dark hair smiled back at him.

"Shit!"

The hairs on the back of his neck stood up and he swallowed hard, but his attention was now diverted. Drifting off the road, James had to break hard, with the car ending up almost in the remains of the garden, on the wide grass verge. Shaken up, he quickly gained some resemblance of composure, reversed the car back and parked up properly on the roadside verge. He tried to calm himself down, running through in his mind that there were no such things as ghosts as he looked back up at the window.

A Ghostly Diversion

The broken glass just stared mockingly back at him.

He got out and quickly examined the cottage for the doorway, deliberately ignoring glancing at the upper windows. There appeared to be no front entrance but on the left-hand side it looked as if there was an overgrown path leading round to the back. He hurried over, followed it, and found the back door stuck partially open but wide enough for him to squeeze past. Heart pounding, he slid through the gap and in the gloom spotted the stairs off to the right.

Summoning up his courage and running up them two at a time he reached the landing and saw the door he thought led into the room he needed. Throwing it open he dashed in and shouted:

"All right, games over, what the hell do you think ..."

The room was empty and glass from the broken window littered the floor. There was no sign that anyone had been there for many years. The wooden floorboards creaked as he stepped on them whilst walking over to the centre of the room and he surveyed the desolate scene spread out before him.

He looked around slowly, but the room was bare, with everything cleared out, the walls though still had some wallpaper on them with some of the exposed under layer suggesting it had once been a girl's room. Wandering back out onto the landing and into the next, slightly larger, room it was just as empty but all the time he had the strangest feeling that he was not alone.

A Ghostly Diversion

The feeling grew steadily, and the air seemed to be turning colder and he involuntarily shivered.

Brave as he thought he was, his courage evaporated, and it was time to leave. He hurried down the stairs again and walked at a quick pace back to the car, his heart pounding. He sat for a few moments but still with the strange cold feeling creeping over him.

He couldn't shake it off.

Finally, it got too much, he started the engine, put the car in gear and drove off down the road before pulling over after a couple of hundred yards just before the outskirts of Grasceby to settle himself down.

"This is getting too much." he muttered and shook his head in disbelief. "Must be a trick of the light, there are *NO* such things as ghosts." He tried to convince himself but somehow the thoughts and words seemed hollow.

He deliberated for a few moments then came to a decision to never to take that route again, his imagination was simply too vivid. He pulled back onto the road and headed for home, his mind still whirling with odd thoughts.

#

She was sad. She'd followed him down and almost to his car but took fright at the last moment before he could see her. For heaven's sake, she's a ghost – shouldn't have let a mortal scare her away like that. The man will probably never come back, and she'll never know why she's felt such hope again after all these years.

A Ghostly Diversion

She returned to her former bedroom and sat at the ghostly base of her once lovely bed gently sobbing to herself whilst idly toying with her little black hair clip in her hair. Dusk fell once more on the cottage and despondency again set in as the light from outside gradually faded as did her hopes.

4: Things that go bump…

Despite his decision, a few days later, James once again found himself taking the diversion. On passing the cottage he couldn't bring himself to look up at the building and drove quickly by. The dark-haired girl felt the passing of his presence that morning and tried something new; she attempted to follow as far as she could, but her spirit was weak and she couldn't keep up. She knew however that something was getting stronger between her and the stranger but when she didn't feel him pass by that early evening, she tried something she'd only done once in the past, and that time she'd failed.

She began to project herself further along the road and forced herself to try to recall where it would lead to. Several times she felt her spirit being pulled back to her home but every time she pushed along a little further. If only she could feel his presence to lock on to, she could try to contact him as she once again came back to the cottage. Try harder she thought and persevere…

#

"Damn! It's happened again!"

Mark was clearly getting annoyed, and James nodded in sympathy.

"It's almost as if those two are failing together in a conspiracy, perhaps they've gone on strike?" James suggested and smiled, trying to lighten the mood but Mark was not having it as he stared back at his colleague. They'd already been there since the office had closed at five thirty p.m., almost three hours earlier.

Patience was wearing a little thin.

A Ghostly Diversion

"Ever since we moved into this dingy place, we've had nothing but trouble – we never had this in London." he complained and sat back on the floor to rest.

"So, who was it who suggested the move up *t'north?*" Asked James knowing he would probably get an earful from his boss and long-time friend.

"Shut it, and for your future reference that's Yorkshire speak, not Lincolnshire!" Mark retorted but had a wry smile on his face as he scowled at James. They were in a funny position as both were trying to fit under a large semi-circular conference desk with built in computer terminals and flat screens, there wasn't much room for two men of average build to be lying underneath it!

James lay down and shuffled further under hoping to be able to reach the backs of the servers and see them both at the same time. His torch flickered and he mused that the last thing he needed was it to go out, now of all times. At least when the computers failed again, he might see something that would give them a clue as to where the problem lay.

For just over a month now everything in the office had worked fine and they had begun to settle down to a more normal routine but this morning, well, it seemed like the gremlins were well and truly back.

"Reboot 'Ops one' then we'll try 'Ops two' and see if they fall over this time." James said underneath the desk in a muffled voice but there was no response from Mark who had got out from under it. James turned and made to get up forgetting momentarily where he was and there was a sickening thud.

A Ghostly Diversion

"@###!!"

Mark peered under the terminal desk "You say something?" then he noticed James holding his head and Mark tried to mask a grin, well at least something had lightened his mood!

James crawled out and warily stood up swaying a little as he did so. He held the upper right side of his head and looked at Mark smirking at him.

"I know you like looking at the stars, but I'm not bothered about seeing them from under there." he muttered as he went off to the washroom to examine the damage and apply a cold compress of wet tissues.

#

The slowly enlarging bump on his forehead was plain to see as James gingerly washed his face and again applied a new cold wet pad of tissues to the bump. He grimaced but as he stared at the damage, he was glad that the skin hadn't been broken. "Helen will just laugh", he reflected to himself in the mirror *"should look what you're doing*, she'll say when I get home – whatever time that will be." He tried to mimic how his wife would look as she said that, but he knew it was a poor impersonation of her.

It was nearly nine p.m. already and he was half an hour later than he'd said when he'd phoned her earlier. He figured the evening meal would probably be in the neighbour's cat or dog, whichever got to it first. He smiled at the thought knowing Helen would never do that, he had to admit she was very patient with him. Still these things were sent to

A Ghostly Diversion

try us he sighed as he wet the cold compress under the cold water tap and applied it again to the bump.

He shivered.

The cold compress probably, he thought shrugging it off.

And shivered again.

Funny, he thought the air conditioning was turned off as there was only Craig, Mark and himself left in the building. Craig was downstairs on the ground floor below them, examining the circuit breakers, electrical feeds, and network cabling. Perhaps one of them had opened the door and just come in to spend a penny – or a pound perhaps - yuk!

An odd feeling came over him and he looked around. There was no one about. 'Must have imagined it', he mused and put a new set of tissues under the cold running tap. Yes, that was it, the cold compress would naturally have the effect, he decided and applied it to his bump again. The pain was subsiding, but he figured it would come out in quite a bruise by morning. Helen would wonder what they had been doing tonight and he smiled to himself.

And shivered again.

But this time it was different.

The room seemed *a lot* cooler now and he felt the hairs on the back of his neck stiffen as if someone was nearby, watching him...

For some reason, he could not fathom, he was suddenly afraid to look up at the mirror and quickly splashed cool water on his face, rubbed it all over then reached over for the towelling he'd found earlier.

Face dried he risked a quick glance up, cursing himself for his lack of courage, but all was still and there was not a soul in the room. But still there was a strong feeling he was not alone.

"Anyone there? Mark? Craig?" he called out, then carefully shook his head at how daft that must have sounded. He looked about slowly at the empty urinals and over to the toilet cubicles, but there was nothing to be seen.

He turned back towards the wash basin and mirror and for a split-second thought he caught something move in the reflection of the cubicles and he spun round.

"For Christ's sake guys stop pissing me about!" he shouted angrily to the cubicles, but there was no one there.

He calmed down.

'Think rationally James', he thought to himself, there's no one here and I've just had a knock on the head. So that's fully explainable, he reassured himself and turned to back to look in the mirror.

Except the dark-haired girl from the cottage now stood staring out at him from the mirror instead of his own reflection and James passed out.

#

"James? James? Come on, old pal, stop frightening us will you!"

James groggily came too and looked up into Mark's anxious face. He was on the floor of the toilet block and both Mark and Craig were clearly worried about him. They bent down and offered hands for him to hold onto to help him get up.

A Ghostly Diversion

"I'm okay, I think." he said slowly as he tried to stand up and swayed a little as the other two held him on either side by his arms. "Where is she?" he asked as he steadied himself and began to realise that he must have passed out.

Mark looked at Craig and shrugged.

"Poor devil must think he's at home" he said, turned back to James, smiled nicely at him and began speaking slowly to him almost like baby talk. " Helen's not here James, you're here at work. We're trying to sort the servers out, but you banged your head, remember?" Mark sounded as if he was talking to a five-year-old and James was about to mutter something obscene in reply when Craig cut in.

"Must have been worse than it looked, we found you passed out by the basin, at least your colour's coming back now though. Lucky for you I'm a first aider!" Craig added and between the two of them they helped James down the corridor back to the main office where he and Mark had been working.

Sitting down James noticed the servers were working at last. "How long have I been out for then?" he asked absentmindedly as he stared at the screens happily scrolling through lots of data.

"'Bout fifteen minutes I reckon." Said Mark scratching his chin thoughtfully. "Craig here came back to tell us he'd found something, and I realised you had been gone a while, so we came looking for you. Must have been quite a bang you gave yourself under there, thought it seemed loud at the time".

"Probably sounded hollow!" Craig quipped, then realised he probably should have kept quiet as the newest and youngest of the team, so he looked down at his shoes. James looked sternly towards Mark then both turned their gaze on Craig who visibly squirmed. Their faces suddenly broke into big grins. Mark slapped him lightly on the back.

"You're probably right there Craig my son!"

It was Craig's turn to break out in a smile now. He knew he liked working with these guys – they were nutters like himself! He felt he was part of a team even though they were both higher up in the company than him and, to be fair, older, and wiser.

James sat and thought about what had happened. Clearly the knock on the head had made him hallucinate and the cold compress had added to matters, so he mentioned nothing more to his colleagues about the girl.

Why worry them needlessly? He thought. Anyway, they'd quite rightly think him mad and feeling the effects of the bang on the head.

So, he kept quiet.

Mark and Craig left him to rest as they went downstairs to collect their tools so they could all leave now the problem servers had been fixed.

James walked back towards the toilets and hesitated briefly. Summoning up the courage he opened the door and quickly looked round inside but there was no cold feeling, and the room was empty. He smiled inwardly, turned, and almost jumped out of his skin as Craig was stood behind him.

"Oops, sorry, Mark says he's ready and waiting to go home so we're to get moving." James nodded and they both walked down the nearby stairs to join Mark to lock up and leave.

A Ghostly Diversion

With the alarm system set as they walked out of the door and onto the gravel of the car park Mark noticed that Craig seemed to be wanting to say something but was clearly uncomfortably with what he wished to say.

"Spit it out then Craig", he said, Craig looked at the two of them and shuffled a little on his feet.

"Err, I was wondering… look I've missed the last bus and wondered if I could be cheeky and get a
lift with one of you?"

Mark briefly looked back at James and noticed he was still touching his head gingerly and he turned back to Craig.

"You're not far from Horncastle are you, Craig?" The younger man nodded, and Mark turned back to James, "Perhaps you could run him home, I'd feel a bit happier knowing you had someone with you as you drive home. Sure, you're feeling up to it?"

James looked up then at the other two and realised what Mark had asked.

"Oh, sure, no problem, where do you live then Craig?"

"Oh, just past a place called Grasceby, it's not too far out of your way I hope." Craig realised that James was staring strangely at him and looked at Mark then back at James, wondering what he'd said.

James shook his head then smiled at him.

"Yep, okay, I know where that is, no problem." He motioned over to his car and Craig nodded and they both got in whilst Mark wandered over to his car and drove off out of the car park at the usual frenetic pace. Luckily the road was quiet as it was late in the evening.

James pulled his phone out of his pocket and with a click was connected to Helen; he quickly explained the even longer delay before he would get home. She was good that there wife of his, he thought, she'd anticipated the delay and would do him a ready meal and chips from the freezer when he got in. 'What a saint', he chuckled to himself as Craig fastened his seatbelt and they drew out of the car park into the misty night.

5: Hit and Run?

Craig didn't realise he was doing it, but after a mile or so James had had enough. Good deed or no good deed, he had to say something.

"What *ARE* you staring at?" James asked.

"Sorry, but, well, I sort of get the feeling that you're not happy taking me home. In fact, it's almost as if Grasceby is the last place you want to go to…" he trailed off and felt he should have kept his mouth shut.

James grimaced but his whole tone changed for the better.

"Oh, look I'm sorry for that. I had a bad experience driving through the village some months ago, so I haven't been that way since. Silly of me and I didn't mean to take it out on you. Let's face it – I'm heading home earlier than I could have been if you hadn't found the problem back there".

Craig relaxed at last and settled down just to watch the road as best he could through the swirling mist.

"How long have you lived in Grasceby then Craig?"

"Oh, just a couple of years really. Moved over from Nottingham, partly to err, get away from my parents. They're a bit demanding you see, always wanting me to settle down and find a girlfriend, not that I haven't been trying. Couldn't find work back home so came over on the promise of an offer of work but it fell through. I was lucky that I have a friend who's away a lot and needed someone to look after and live in his home whilst they're away, so it looks lived in and not deserted.

Glad I got the job with you folks as I was beginning to run out of savings, still have to pay some rent but at least it's not onerous! What about you?"

"Oh, we're originally from Albury near Guildford. Pretty much lived all my life there except for university at Aston where I met Mark. Mark got work at the firm we're at today and recommended me to them and the rest is history as they say. Married Helen over twenty years ago but no kids … and don't ask…"

By now it was after 9:30p.m. and the skies were quite dark as they were into September. A reddish, not quite full, moon appeared to be rising low over on the eastern side of the sky giving some extra light. There was patchy mist hanging about, in some places it appeared quite dense and for a moment Craig wondered if James was going too fast.

He seemed to be a good driver though, certainly in control, so he settled back down again, and they discussed the company, the recent problems at work, more of his own background and annoyance at not finding a woman who'll have him, and his dreams for the future.

The mist hung more densely now in places and seemed to be gradually thickening. After taking the turning at Wragby, James accidentally overshot the turning that would take them towards Grasceby. Apologising, he found a driveway a short distance down the road and quickly turned back, slowing in order to spot the lane before they overshot it again. This time he got it right and once again they were on

A Ghostly Diversion

course. After a couple of miles, the road reached a familiar section with the entrance to the disused airfield then a sharp bend and the line of trees began on the left side.

James didn't notice though as he was now in full conversation about his Florida holiday a few weeks back and the excitement at seeing a rocket blast off from the Kennedy Space Centre. The mist began to swirl around the car, denser now, so James slowed a little trying to keep to the road. Flicking a switch, he found the fog lights he'd cleaned the other day, now gave a slightly better view, but even so he hadn't realised he was still doing almost forty miles per hour.

Suddenly without warning, amongst the denser patches of mist, a female figure with long flowing hair and her back to him loomed quickly into view on the left side partially on the road. Startled, he swerved violently to the right to avoid her but to James it seemed she touched the left side of the front of the car bonnet, and he shouted as the car veered and screeched to a halt at an angle across the road.

Craig virtually jumped out of his skin as he had seen nothing except mist; he didn't have time to think about it as the car came to an abrupt halt. James shouted about a girl, leapt out of the car, and was rushing off back down the road. Craig quickly undid his seat belt and scrambled out, not quite knowing what to expect.

James came to a halt after several metres, almost out of breath, as he kept apologising into the mist for not paying attention and hoping she was all right.

He looked around.

A Ghostly Diversion

The mist continued to swirl about him, and he frantically searched the roadside for what should have been the body of the girl. He listened for any kind of groaning from someone injured but there was nothing at all.

"Anybody there?
Someone?
Are you hurt?"

He kept shouting but gradually trailed off when there was no reply.

No sign of anyone, in fact.

The mist had taken on a strange eerie red form due to the car's rear lights in the distance. It flowed around him as he looked round trying to make sense of the last few moments. He shook his head and slowly made his way back to the car – barely visible in the distance with its rear red lights glowing in the mist. He noted a shaken Craig stood next to the open passenger side door. Along the way James kept looking at the roadside and listening but to no avail. As he approached, Craig looked at him strangely.

"What was it? Did you find them?" He asked and James felt a surge of relief, at least he hadn't imagined it then if Craig had also seen the girl.

"No – so you saw her too then?" he answered but this time Craig tilted his head at James quizzically.

"Err, who?"

James didn't expect this.

"Well, the young woman of course! Thought I'd clipped her as I saw her too late in the misty headlights."

Craig patted him on the shoulder.

A Ghostly Diversion

"I really didn't see anything – I was talking to you and looking your way when you suddenly shouted about someone in the road and then you swerved, and we came to a halt. There was no bump or feeling we hit anything at all".

He looked up at James's head and the raised bump. "Hope you don't mind me saying this, but I reckon that bump you took was a bit more serious than we originally thought".

James shook his head in dismay although that made his head seem to spin a little and he stopped. He gestured with both hands at Craig.

"Look I know what I saw and for a second it was as if someone came out of the mist, and I really thought we'd hit them. Perhaps it was a deer or something – there's some the other side of Horncastle you know, near Scrawlsby-"

"*Scrivelsby*" corrected Craig and he moved round to the front of the car in full view of the headlights and bent down to examine them.

James joined him and they checked the front left side of the car but there was nothing to suggest they had hit anything except plenty of insect and moth bodies splattered across the lights. Up ahead, very dimly, a pair of headlights drifted into view and James quickly got back into the car, reversed it on to the proper side of the road and parked up. Craig stood at the verge side of the road and silently worried about his colleague.

A dark green Range Rover drew up beside them with the driver winding down his window.

"You all right there?" came the rich Lincolnshire dialect.

A Ghostly Diversion

"Err yes fine mate, mist was a bit thick, I'm sort of new to the area and thought I'd lost the road." Replied James a little hesitantly. The driver leaned out of his window and looked at both Craig and James, eyeing them up. Craig leaned over to speak.

"Get many deer around these parts at this time of year mate?" Craig asked.

'Good question' thought James and the other driver smiled at them thoughtfully.

"Aye we do that – get out and go a roaming at this time o' year, rutting season you know – makes them do all sorts o' things." He revved his engine and was about to drive off, but he kept looking at James as if he'd seen someone familiar. James tried to smile but, in his heart, he knew that he wasn't convincing as he was struggling to get the image of the girl in the mist out of his mind. The driver looked at both of them again and put the Range Rover into first gear ready for the off.

"Hope you don't mind me saying so but if you're to ask me I'd say you'd seen a ghost! Pale as owt you are!" He chuckled to himself and with that he gunned the engine and drove off down the road to be enveloped by the thickening mist, his tail lights fading into the distance.

James coughed and swallowed hard as a thought occurred to him. He turned to face Craig again. "Just bear with me while I check something out will you - and promise not to say anything to Helen if you meet her – OK?"

Puzzled, Craig nodded silently, and James got in the car and parked the car further up onto the grass verge and got out. Something was stirring inside him, and he had to know. He walked back

A Ghostly Diversion

down the road and passed where he had stopped earlier in his frantic search for the 'person'.

He carried on a little further as the red rear lights slowly faded away into the swirling mist.

The tree line pulled away from the roadside after a few more metres and James's heart started pounding harder. Several more metres and there, off to one side swirling in the drifting mist, stood the abandoned cottage, dark, lonely, and forbidding.

"Damn!"

He shuddered and then heard Craig calling to him. He stared at the windows, especially at the upper left hand one and froze as he saw her looking out sad and lonely before she faded away.

Stunned and confused he turned on his heels and headed back to the car.

Craig was getting impatient now.

"James! What the hell is going on?"

Turning to Craig he realised they should be back on the road and getting home. He looked at his younger colleague and managed a brief smile.

"I reckon you're probably right, knock on the head didn't put any sense into me did it! Sorry for that – I think I must be feeling the aftereffects. Come on let's get you home." Without another word between them they got in, James put the car in gear and in silence they carried on down the road as Craig gave him directions to his home.

#

She felt him recede into the distance but with someone else with him she knew the circumstances were not right. Once again, she'd been re-living the fateful moments of her last day when, unexpectedly, he'd almost driven through her. Her spirit had been disrupted briefly until she could collect herself together again.

By then it was too late and typically the chance had been missed. She drifted through the cottage, back up to her old room and longed for an answer to her prayers as the enveloping mist drifted through the broken windows to give her company as she realised too late, he had been standing there looking at her as she wandered back to her bed.

She looked out again, but he was gone and the mist swirled even more thickly hiding the road from her.

6: 'Wolds View' Cottage

Helen was becoming concerned. Over the last few weeks her husband had started acting a little strangely. Normally James was the sort of guy who took most things in his stride and often laughed problems off. But recently his mood had changed and she'd occasionally caught a hint of something in him, especially after they had passed a certain left hand turning at Wragby on their way to one of their occasional big shopping trips to Lincoln.

She didn't want to think of the possibility, but she knew that at some point she would have to know the truth. Or, at the very least, try to get to the bottom of whatever seemed to be on his mind.

Was he having an affair?

She shuddered at the thought and knew that it would be completely out of character for him to do such a thing – but what else could it be? If she tried to steer the subject towards a hint of what she was thinking, then he became dismissive and just disarmingly smiled his way off the topic, making her even more suspicious.

The other night when he had come home late from the office with a bump on his head, she had to admit to herself she'd thought perhaps his other 'love' had hit him for some unknown reason. He certainly seemed evasive about what had kept him so much later than he'd expected; when she happened to see Craig in town by accident the next day, he too seemed to avoid mentioning the previous night. She sighed and reluctantly decided to keep a check on him as much as she could, feeling guilty of even the

A Ghostly Diversion

thought of having to do so. Helen truly hoped she had got things wrong, but the nagging doubts remained to tease and torment her.

Whatever it was, something was clearly haunting him. Little did she know how true that really was. That night James had woken up in a cold sweat and she could have sworn she heard him say in his sleep something about 'who was she' and 'come back to me'. Surely that was the telling moment when she should have confronted him, but she just couldn't do it at that moment.

It was Sunday and he had said the previous day that he was popping down to see Craig, but when she saw Craig later that afternoon in town, he was sketchy as to what they'd been up to and that had chilled her more. Helen needed a little more time to come to terms with her thoughts and now James had gone out – 'to see Craig'. She sat in their living room and looked out of the bay window into the sky, watching the flecks of clouds drift by in the bright sunshine and sighed not knowing what to think or do.

#

It was time, he thought to himself, to have another look. James drove through the village of Grasceby and along the now familiar road. Once again, up ahead, he could just see the clearing where the cottage stood, and he warily pulled up on the grass verge outside it bordering the overgrown garden. Taking a deep breath, he looked up at the windows – but saw nothing.

A Ghostly Diversion

He wasn't sure whether to be relived or annoyed.

Craig stepped out of the car and looked at the cottage with a wary eye. When James had told him everything on Saturday morning he really began to worry about his colleague. Especially when James again insisted not to say a word if by any chance Craig saw Helen. That had been awkward when by accident he'd bumped into her in Horncastle marketplace that afternoon. But James was quite insistent and so here they were – about to look round what surely must be somebody's property – even if it was abandoned and somewhat run down.

James had already gone round the back now and suddenly Craig felt alone and quickly hurried round to join him.

Scared?

Him?

No, of course not!

Well not really, he thought. He considered it a wild goose chase, but better humour James for the time being, he decided. He was sure James had probably been concussed the other night in the mist but when he suggested the idea James had argued vociferously that he was all right; the events involving the 'ghost' had started well before the knock on the head. By now James was already inside the cottage and Craig hurried to catch up with him.

James walked up the stairs and carefully opened the door to the bedroom he'd gone into a few weeks earlier. The room was almost bare, with glass everywhere which looked like it came from the broken windows. "Probably the local kids" he said to himself and walked over to the window and looked out.

His car was in view and parked on the verge just at the edge of the overgrown garden and concrete slab path. He knew the room seemed cold and indeed the whole cottage had what he could only describe as a sad air to it. Perhaps it was the musty smell that seemed to persist throughout it he thought, trying to stop his imagination taking over.

Footsteps galloped up the stairs and he turned quickly, heart racing, but it was only Craig. *Daft, as if a ghost would make so much noise* he thought and shook his head slightly. He didn't blame his younger friend for having doubts about him. He'd doubt his story if he hadn't experienced the ghostly views of the girl over the last few months!

Craig smiled nervously at him then turned and went out of the room, across the landing and into the next slightly bigger room.

"James!"

Hearing his name called out suddenly startled him and he walked quickly out onto the landing and across into the other room to find Craig peeling back some of the wallpaper.

"Thought you weren't too keen on coming into someone else's property? Now I find you pulling the wall apart!" said James and Craig just shrugged and pointed to what he had found.

"Look at this!"

There were a couple of layers of wallpaper, but they hid a layer that seemed to consist of very faded and almost disintegrating newspaper clippings stuck up on the wall.

A Ghostly Diversion

James carefully helped peel some more back, but in doing so, suddenly the plaster gave way and pulled off the wall taking most of the clippings with it. "Damn! That's probably why they papered over the clippings rather than try to remove them." James shook his head and he and Craig knelt to see what they could salvage just as the room took on a different feel and to go really cold.

James shuddered.

He knew they were no longer alone.

He looked at Craig who suddenly realised he was being watched and he glanced back at James with a quizzical look.

"What?"

"Don't you feel it?" James said quietly as he looked around waiting for something, half suspecting what that something would be.

"Er – cold but then the windows are smashed so that's not surprising and it is the end of September." He answered but he too had felt the sudden change in temperature and now James's ghost story was suddenly not so unreal or daft sounding after all.

He got to his feet clutching a shred of the newspaper that was no longer stuck to the plaster. "This looks interesting, we'll see more perhaps with better light outside."

With that he made for the doorway but realised James was not following. "You coming?" he asked and felt a ripple of cold pass over him. He didn't wait for an answer, and he found himself rushing down the stairs, out into the early autumn sunshine, anything to get away from the room.

A Ghostly Diversion

James turned to go and felt a wave of coldness pass over him too. He was determined not to run and turned round...

She stood staring at the wall they had just ruined then turned to him as his veins turned to ice and James was rooted to the spot. He started breathing heavily and couldn't speak but as he looked at her smiling at him, he knew he had to stay. She was a pretty, quite young-looking lass; long black hair with a small black hair clip on one side keeping it tidy and in place, hazel eyes and a dimple on her right cheek. Dressed in what looked like something from the nineteen fifties with a quite low-cut blue top and summery looking long skirt with flowers all over it. She didn't speak but looked back at the wall and then back at him and smiled and nodded. He blinked and then she was gone.

"CRAIG!!!"

James bellowed at the top of his voice and for a few moments he thought Craig had run off and left him completely alone. But then hesitant footsteps came up the stairs and Craig gingerly looked round the door. White faced, James looked as if he had seen a ghost and Craig shuddered at the thought.

"She appeared to me again. Right there, right there on that spot" James spoke the words carefully as he pointed downwards and thought about what he had seen. "She looked at the wall and where the newspaper clippings had been fixed and she looked at me and smiled before vanishing."

He swallowed before going on and some resolve came back to him. He stepped closer to Craig. "Something happened here, we're on to something Craig, I know it now. I'm sure she doesn't mean me

A Ghostly Diversion

or you any harm – there's something that happened here and it's unfinished, I'm sure of it!"

Craig himself swallowed hard and couldn't deny that something did indeed seem strange about the cottage. But his thoughts kept turning back to the bump on James's forehead and there was still a flicker of doubt in his mind. Still, the clippings he had in his hands were certainly strange and had piqued his interest.

"Come down and have a look at this will you?"

He turned and left the room – a bit more calmly than the last time. James followed, for a brief moment he looked back hoping to see the girl again, but the room remained bare as his thoughts churned away. She seemed to be telling him something about the cottage, that's for sure. He walked down the stairs, stepped out the back door into the weak sunshine and into the rough, overgrown garden as he followed the path into the sunlight.

The overlying layers of wallpaper had done much damage to the newspaper clippings, and they were really just fragments. However, what they could clearly see however, was a faded picture of a distraught man holding a picture of what looked like a young girl. Part of the headline was visible: 'Distraught Father appe...'. The rest was lost – probably still stuck on the wall. James held the clipping gingerly and tried to angle it to get the light on it better and it began to fragment even more. He could see though the picture of the girl.

"*That's her* – the girl I've seen here!" James said quietly, almost as if to nobody as his thoughts became more focused. There was no doubt now that something had happened here and somehow, he had triggered her to appear to him. Craig was leaning over his shoulder quietly. "Well, what do you think now Craig?" Craig stepped back with a frown across his face.

"I dunno, it's weird all right. Up to now I could have sworn it was down to that there bang on the head you got the other night."

"But you see what I've been getting at this morning when I told you about what I'd seen? Surely now it's beginning to come together. The only thing that gets me is just that, why me? I'm not even from Lincolnshire, let alone Grasceby."

Craig looked up at the cottage not wanting to see anything strange and he was glad that it just looked as it appeared – an empty and quite lonely property.

"I wonder who actually owns this place? Seems strange to me that for somewhere with what looks to be a good sound structure it hasn't been snapped up and modernised?" He said and James nodded in agreement.

"Precisely my thoughts as well." He looked the cottage over again. "If a girl did vanish from here and was either found dead or is still missing then I'm not sure I would want to live here – that's if the estate agent mentioned the full facts!" He said wryly. Craig looked thoughtfully at his shoes and bent down to tie them up. He looked back up at James.

"You know it might be worth popping back to the other side of the village to the inn – you know the 'Star and Crescent Moon' a mile or so out, what do you think? There could be someone there who might give us some background."

A Ghostly Diversion

James smiled, nodded in agreement, and looked back at the cottage. At least now he was warmer, and the pervading chill had gone.

"Probably best not to mention what I've seen or even the fact that we've been in the property – might not go down too well if we happen to discover who owns the place. I'd hate to be done for trespassing!" Craig nodded and they both walked through the rough grass and got into the car.

#

She watched the car drive off towards the village and felt a small measure of satisfaction. Perhaps the man she now knew as James would be able to help her continue on to the next life and leave this sad world of hers forever.

He was nice and seemed familiar and he didn't appear quite so afraid this time – although she doubted his younger friend would have hung around if she'd appeared before he had left the room!

Perhaps it was only a matter of time before he came back on his own and she settled down in her room to wait for him to return with a renewed sense of hope.

7: The Star and Crescent Moon Inn

Quaint!

They pulled into the car park and studied the Inn for several minutes. The 'Star and Crescent Moon' inn looked to be a couple of centuries old at least, with plenty of ivy along with other plants growing up the walls of the building adding to its attractive appearance. It had clearly been extended in the last twenty years as the modern looking conservatory style section off to one side attested to. They could see neatly laid out tables inside with several couples seated having a meal and it did look quite cosy.

The inn was set in almost an acre of land with hedges and trees surrounding it on three sides with the fourth side giving a grand view to the southwest. The gravel car park looked reasonably fresh suggesting a new layer of gravel had been applied in the last few months.

"Wonder how old it is?" Craig said aloud opening the car door and getting out. There were some flecks of cloud about in the sky now, he straightened his jacket and buttoned up the front. James's attention was momentarily distracted though as he spied a familiar blue Mercedes parked over in the corner of the car park. He mentally noted the registration number just in case, as his mind wandered a little remembering it was the Mercedes that had led him to go past the cottage in the first place all those months ago.

He realised what Craig had asked and looked back at the inn.

A Ghostly Diversion

"I'm no expert but perhaps eighteenth or nineteenth century? Could even be older as it has clearly been added to over the years." he replied as he joined his colleague. They walked over to what appeared to be the front entrance with a sign hanging over the door.

"'Marcus Crabb. Licensed to sell intoxicating liquor and alcoholic beverages'. Well at least we know who the owner is." Stated Craig.

James nodded and, opening the door, stepped in. His eyes had to quickly adapt from the bright sunshine outside to the more dimly lit interior, but he was pleased to see it was a warm and friendly setting. Half a dozen men of various ages were off to the right at a table having a laugh at some story one of them had told. A relatively young couple were arm in arm at the bar supping their drinks, they turned as James and Craig came in.

"Good God, James – what brings you out here?" Asked the tall man.

"And where's Helen?" The young lady called over to them and James realised they were a couple that he and Helen had met in Horncastle not long after they had moved up to the area. He hadn't seen them for a few weeks and didn't realise they were locals to the inn.

He smiled and went over to them.

"Oh, she's at home" he replied to the lady, and he looked behind towards his friend and motioned at Craig, "Craig, this is David and Terri." He looked back at them "Craig's a colleague of mine from work who lives nearby." They all nodded at each other and smiled. James noted their glasses were virtually empty. "Are you two ready for a top up?" He offered.

David sipped down the last dregs of his beer and smiled at James.

"Sorry but you're a bit late, we're almost ready to get off down to a charity fête over at Wragby. But I'll remind you next time, eh?"

Terri smiled, finished her orange juice, put the glass down and swung her handbag across her shoulder ready to depart.

"Tell Helen I'm surprised she let you out – I must have words with her – can't let you men go wandering around the countryside without someone to keep you under control!" She laughed, shuffled the bag strap up higher, turned to David and mentioned something to him in his ear that James couldn't catch.

"Oh, yeah, good idea. James when you and your good lady are free why not come over to ours for a meal sometime?" James nodded his approval, and the couple bade farewell and left.

Then he shook his head.

"Damn, I could have asked them about the cottage!" He said as the barmaid came past picking up glasses and looked at James expectantly.

"Oh, right," he turned to his friend "what do you want then Craig?" Craig looked along the bar and up at the various bar taps before ordering a pint of Batemans and James followed suit. A short wait: they got their drinks and sat at the bar idly chatting and debating who they should approach for information – they didn't want to look to be busybodies.

A Ghostly Diversion

James turned to Craig looking puzzled. "You live just a couple of miles away - you don't know anything then?"

Craig just shrugged.

"Remember I've only been here a couple of years but never really noticed the cottage before - don't get the heebie jeebies like you when I go past it!"

James mockingly grimaced at Craig and continued to look round. Finally, a more elderly gentleman appeared behind the bar and James decided to try his luck. Getting up, he approached the barman and got his attention.

"Excuse me, I hope you don't mind me asking, but I'm looking over the area for properties for clients and noticed an abandoned cottage on the other side of the village about a mile or so out. Slightly offset from the road. Do you know who owns it?"

The barman looked at him with a funny, knowing sort of smile and had a little chuckle to himself. He put a newly dried glass back up on the shelf behind him then placed his hands firmly on the bar surface and looked James squarely in the face.

"Guess you mean 'Wolds View', eh?"

James smiled inwardly to himself - another piece of the puzzle falls into place perhaps, he hoped.

"The one with trees on the north side of the road, before you get to a small clearing between them and the cottage. There are fields the other side of the road and I think there's a large set of farm buildings a bit further on."

The barman looked at him with barely a flicker of emotion.

A Ghostly Diversion

"Sounds 'bout right. Won't be for sale though. Haven't seen it on the market for donkey's years now, probably never will."

James looked at him questioningly, but the barman just smiled at him.

"Err, sorry, have I missed something?"

"Nope."

The barman looked at him and turned away to tend to a customer who'd just inconveniently come up to be served. The conversation had suddenly dried up and James didn't quite know where to take it but decided to persist when the barman became free again a few minutes later.

"Well, my clients are not exactly poor, and it would seem an ideal location, is there someone I can talk to or get in contact with, so I can follow it up?" He asked hoping to get a bit more from the barman. The chap looked a little disgruntled and briefly looked over to the group of men at the table then back at James. He turned back to the group.

"Fred, FRED! Bloke here wants to know about 'Wolds View' – doesn't seem to understand it's not for sale". The more elderly of the group looked up disparagingly, annoyed that his lunchtime get-together with his pals was being disturbed. He looked James and Craig over as they shuffled uncomfortably on their seats, and he leaned back in his chair.

"City blokes then?" He suddenly asked and didn't wait for a reply, "Could do with leaving the local properties for the local people if you ask me".

James felt like answering back but bit his tongue.

"That may be the case but I'm only doing some research, if it's so much bother to you then I'll be on my way. Any commission that might have come your way I get to keep 'cause I'll get the info one way or another." James bluffed and turned to go, startling Craig who was now seeing another side to his colleague. 'Fred' got up and started toward them.

"Now wait up there fella, let's not be hasty. No offence meant but you don't get many folks asking about that cottage that's all. Come over here and we can have a drink?" He motioned to one side away from his original pals, turning to them, "Won't be long chaps – keep me seat warm and don't you DARE look at me cards, especially you Eric!"

He cast a brief glance towards the back of the room to a solitary figure then came forward towards James.

The three of them sat down near the side window overlooking the car park and the barman came over to them with a disapproving expression on his face. Fred looked up at him.

"Marcus, I'll have the usual – what about you guys?" James looked at the barman he'd been talking to earlier and realised he was the owner of the inn. They raised their still almost full glasses and politely declined. He turned to Fred as Marcus headed back behind the bar.

"Anyway – who can I contact concerning this cottage?"

For some reason Fred looked about and especially over to the far corner again where James realised a lone drinker was sitting quietly. He didn't seem to be paying anybody much attention until he looked at James and for a moment seemed to freeze,

A Ghostly Diversion

before bringing his glass up to his lips and averting James' gaze.

"Wolds View's a nice place to a certain extent but I'd be surprised if the owners are even bothered about selling at any price."

James looked at him and smiled.

"If the price is right then no one in their right mind could refuse, it would have to be something pretty drastic to stop them making a tidy sum." He offered.

Fred looked at him warily and dropped his eyes to his glass.

"You might just be right about that last bit mate. However, that place has got a bit of history." He hesitated before continuing. "Must be more'n fifty years now I guess." He looked down again then back over to the other chap in the corner, who seemed to be eyeing them up.

"Since what?" Craig asked impatiently and Fred looked over at them both.

"All I'll say is that you'd be hard pressed to get anyone to go near that place. They reckon it's haunted yer see and the last people who rented it left in a rush and we haven't seen them since. That was, oh, at least thirty years now itself. Look mate I wouldn't bother with it and leave it be."

With that Fred got up just as Marcus arrived with Fred's order and Fred took it off the tray. "Thanks for the drink." and tipped the glass slightly towards James in thanks as he went back over to his mates to their happy cheers and good-humoured laughter.

James looked at Craig, Marcus leaned over and presented the bill.

A Ghostly Diversion

"I guess I'm getting that." James realised and paid him. Marcus turned to go then turned back to them.

"See what I mean – not worth the hassle mate. Have a good day." He sloped off and went back to the bar to clean the slops spilled on the surface. Craig rocked back and forth in his chair, and they supped their drinks as they digested what had been said, which was precious little when they mulled it over.

Pint finally finished, James got up, motioned to Craig to follow and they went out into the car park. He turned at the doorway though sensing something and at first, he thought it was Fred and his mates. Fred smiled over and raised his glass but then James realised he was being watched and he looked over towards the back-left hand side.

Straight into the eyes of the chap in the corner who had now been joined by Marcus. James quickly turned away, stepped outside and blinked in the sunshine as he made his way over to his car and Craig, who seemed in deep thought.

"Well, that seems to settle one thing." He said and James looked at him questioningly. "You've stumbled on something that's for sure, they certainly weren't keen on giving anything away, were they?"

James nodded, unlocked the car with his smart phone, whilst lost in his own thoughts.

Craig continued. "I tell you what though James,"

James looked up across the roof of the car.

"I'd tell Helen. You're right – there is something strange to all this, but I wouldn't keep her in the dark, she might be able to help you."

James nodded as they got into the car and he drove Craig back to his home before heading for home himself, deep in thought.

#

Back at the inn, Marcus cleared the solitary glass from the table and for a moment there was an empty silence
from his customer and long-time friend, Richard.

"What was that all 'bout then?" Richard finally asked and Marcus shrugged and looked squarely into the other man's face.

"Some sort of property dealer – spotted 'Wolds View' and asked about it." He replied and Richard frowned.

"'Suppose someone'll eventually buy it, but bet it won't be long before it's empty again." He grimaced as he thought about the cottage and memories came flooding back, painful echoes of an almost forgotten time when he had thought the world was his for the taking. Then someone he loved disappeared from both the cottage and his life and things had never been the same again.

Apart from a couple of brief visits he had never been back, certainly not inside, but he was never keen on anyone else 'invading' that property. He glanced out the side window and could just see the chap talking to his friend across the roof of the car and then they got in and drove off. Fortunately, it turned away from the direction they would have taken if going back to 'Wolds View' and he relaxed a little.

A Ghostly Diversion

Forcing a brief smile at Marcus he got up, settled his bill, and left the inn. He walked over to his metallic blue Mercedes and got in. As he reached the main road, just briefly, very briefly, he almost turned towards the direction of the cottage but changed his mind at the last minute and headed for his home in Horncastle instead.

8: A lonely walk...

James didn't tell her.

He didn't know how to start explaining to Helen what he had experienced over the last few months and so tried to continue his life as normally as possible. He hadn't really found out much at all at the inn except the locals clearly thought the cottage was haunted, but they were reluctant to say any more. He wasn't sure of his next move and although Craig now seemed to believe him there were moments when he had begun to doubt himself.

He also realised that work itself was beginning to suffer and Mark had started making one or two slightly cryptic but snide comments recently. So, James avoided the cottage until he could decide what he should do, if anything at all. Over the following week Craig kept asking him quietly whether he had made any progress and James kept giving excuses to him but at some stage he knew he was going to have to find out what had happened at 'Wolds View' especially what happened to the girl he'd seen.

But not yet.

Or so he thought.

He left the car park at work that evening fully intending to simply drive straight home via the main road but as he neared Wragby he felt something strange inside. It was almost as if he was compelled to turn off the main road and head in a certain direction.

But at the traffic lights he overcame the feeling and to the annoyance of a car to his left, as the lights changed, he quickly accelerated and cut back in front of the other car instead of taking the turnoff he'd originally signalled to take.

He fervently hoped it hadn't been an unmarked police car as he sped away or that there was no CCTV looking down at the traffic lights. A mile down the road though, he suddenly found himself taking a side road he'd never been on before and his heart began racing. Almost three miles later as he drove along the tiny single-track road, he eventually came out at the road he would have been on if he'd turned at the traffic lights and he instinctively turned left.

He knew where he was going, and the compulsion seemed even stronger now. The sign for Grasceby appeared up ahead and again he tried to convince himself to drive on to the next village but to no avail as he indicated and turned left again. The sharp bend and the start of the tree line on his left meant he was close and sure enough he automatically slowed down as the clearing appeared on his left...

...and there was 'Wolds View' silently waiting for him standing in the clearing almost as if it was aloof, defying him to enter.

Quiet.

Empty, just like the pit of his stomach, James thought as he pulled onto the grass verge that merged with the overgrown garden attached to the cottage, but before the tree line began again.

He looked warily at it, realising that it would soon be dark. He got out of the car and slowly walked tentatively round to the rear entrance. The air was damp, and the sky was overcast as he walked

A Ghostly Diversion

along the overgrown path and it started to drizzle. He pulled his collar up and pushed the door open uneasily. Peering in, his eyes adjusted to the gloom, but everything was quiet. He'd never actually looked round the ground floor and so he stepped over some rubble on the floor and walked through what looked like the kitchen into the front room.

Nothing. Cleared out completely. It was also eerily dark as the downstairs windows were in most parts boarded up but with a few slats fallen off, exposing some of the room to a little light.

"Empty, just like upstairs", he said to no one and went over to the dust covered mantelpiece above the fireplace. It was a long time since it had seen the flickering flames of a fire and he looked round at the dirty walls. What little wallpaper was left was peeling off and littering the floor but there was nothing like the clippings he and Craig had found upstairs a few weeks before.

A side door led into what could have been the living room and it too was suffering from the many years of the neglect that surrounded 'Wolds View' cottage. The drizzle outside was drifting in through a gap in the boardings of the broken windows and he shivered involuntarily.

A sound!

Something fell onto the floor upstairs and he froze, suddenly wishing he wasn't there.

Silence.

Perhaps it was nothing more than a mouse or a rat, he tried to tell himself and summoned up the courage to venture upstairs.

He walked back through into the kitchen. Back into the hallway and noticed the light switch.

A Ghostly Diversion

He tried it but no power, so he then headed up the stairs, his footsteps quite noisy in the silence of the cottage and he felt guilty disturbing it and possibly whatever it was he was reluctantly seeking.

Into the right-hand room, he looked around but in the dim gloom there was nothing to be seen. Across now into the second larger room where the clippings had been. On the floor was part of the remains of the plaster that had come away when Craig and he had tried to examine them closer. There was the answer as ...a small part of the plaster dropped to the floor in front of him as if it had been flicked out by an invisible hand.

It added to the small pile on the desolate floor.

He smiled inwardly and shook his head turning to go, noting it was getting cold...

She stood between him and the door.

Startled, he stepped back and looked round – silly really, as there was only the one way out, but she just looked at him with her sad hazel eyes and he forced himself to calm down.

"O...OK – who are you then?"

He managed to find the words and she sadly smiled at him, pointed her hand to her throat as if to say she couldn't speak, then pointed her right hand towards him and motioned with her fingers and nodded for him to follow. Rooted to the spot, he realised he could partially see through her, as if she were semi-transparent and he shivered at that realisation.

She walked out the doorway and seemed to drift down the stairs and, after the initial shock, James suddenly found he was following her.

A Ghostly Diversion

Through the kitchen and out the back door, round into the garden and then past his car, (through it in fact as he watched!) then out onto the road. His mouth was dry, but he knew he had to follow her. Craig should be seeing this, he thought briefly, then realised that Craig had not seen her when he'd been here with him the last time.

He had felt cold though and that did seem to indicate that she was near on those occasions.

He was certainly cold now.

And wet.

The drizzle had increased, and he thought about opening the car and getting his coat. But he was becoming mesmerised by this young mysterious girl or young woman, and he just had to find out what she was trying to show him.

He had an idea and suddenly stopped and waited, wondering if she could feel his presence and would come back for him. But she carried on walking, or was that actually drifting, he wondered, as her feet didn't seem to quite touch the ground. She carried along the left side of the road leaving him behind. He hurried to catch up but stayed a few metres back from her. Just as he caught up, she turned and briefly looked at him with those soft sad eyes.

He couldn't help thinking that in another time and place she would have been quite a catch, but he stopped himself – he was happily married, and this thought brought a pang of guilt as he wondered what anyone would make of this, especially Helen.

A grown man following a ghostly girl to heaven knows where! And for that matter she did

A Ghostly Diversion

look quite young, and her clothes gave the impression of a precocious teenager. In fact, he realised they were the same clothes as the last time he'd seen her. More to the point, he now realised she was always in the same clothes, perhaps the ones she'd died in …

He shivered at the thought.

She again stopped and appeared to wait for him to get a little closer, then she appeared to step into the undergrowth between the trees and disappeared from his sight.

Panicking he caught up and reached the same spot and looked into the gloom in the slim gap of the tree line.

Barely noticeable, there was something which could have been an overgrown path leading away across the field towards the small wood. He stepped through the undergrowth, watching his feet carefully as he had thought there was a ditch along this side of the road.

It was dark in there but only for a moment, he could see her emerge into the dull evening light. The wood was quite thin in width but followed the road for almost a mile either side of the cottage before petering out.

She waited for him to catch up again and then resumed her journey moving along the faded path which now cut across a field of what had been wheat just the other month. In the distance the field sloped gently down then rose just as gently up towards what looked, from his position, like a long slight ridge across his line of sight, 'probably a field boundary' he thought to himself.

She turned again to watch him, then carried on.

This was the longest he had ever seen the girl and his heartbeat faster as he wondered how she must have died. He shook his head to get the horrible thoughts out of his mind but realised he was being daft; she was a ghost! She had to be dead, otherwise he wouldn't see her like this. Late nineteen fifties era he thought, had to be, as he looked at her long summery dress and somewhat revealing blue top and decided that he should hurry up as she seemed to be leaving him behind.

He was getting soaked now and suddenly sneezed and she abruptly stopped and looked round at him. He looked back at her and saw she actually looked worried, and he found himself waving her on and he picked up his pace. James couldn't find it within him though to catch up and be beside her, preferring to stay a few paces behind.

He knew that it all seemed surreal, but he also knew there was surely a point to this little trek across the field. He couldn't help but think that just a few months ago he'd have thought he was mad following a ghost, especially considering he didn't believe in such things.

Not any more, he reflected.

Not when you are following one to heaven knows where!

They reached the slight ridge and James realised that it was an overgrown drainage ditch stretching away into the distance on either side. He realised it was running almost parallel to the road which now lay almost half a mile away on one side and a wooded stretch close to the north. It was pretty much overgrown so clearly no longer in good condition and unused.

She now turned and walked off along the ditch to the left. He became aware in the gloom that further along there were signs that a small bridge once spanned the gap across the drain, and she drifted over it as if it was still there and started walking back along the other side. Trying to keep his eyes on her he slipped and just caught his balance as she turned back to watch him.

Seeing nowhere to cross he stayed on the south side of the ditch and followed her progress but then she stopped, looked straight into his eyes, and somehow drifted/fell down the side of the drain. He had to blink as the raindrops were now running in rivulets down his forehead into his eyes, but she had disappeared into the ditch side and was gone.

He waited.

Ten minutes.

Twenty. He was getting drenched, cold, and shivering but there was still no sign of her. In the distance, off to the right amongst the gathering gloom, a mechanical digger sat idly by further down the ditch and he realised that it was part of the on-going restoration of the drainage system around there.

James was not interested in it though as he felt his shivering was getting worse and he sneezed loudly. He looked along the bank where she'd vanished but there was nothing to see except grass and he shrugged his shoulders in despair.

Half an hour and he had to give up as the rain came down and the sky became darker. He struggled to find the old path across the fields, back

A Ghostly Diversion

through the now almost pitch-black thin wood and then back onto the road. He was grateful to get to the car as the sneezing fits increased, he fumbled with the electronic car key and the engine spluttered into life.

Heater full on he looked into the rear-view mirror and saw his soaked reflection and he wondered how he was going to explain this to Helen as he drove off down the road shaking his head.

#

She watched him drive off from her bedroom window. If only she could speak, she could tell him everything and it would be over. But if it had been that simple, she might have convinced the young couple decades ago to help instead of scaring them away.

But no. She hadn't shown him everything as she realised, he was drenched from head to toe. All she could do was hope that James didn't die of pneumonia and join her before his time…

She needed him.

She needed someone to find out at last what had happened to her all those years ago and to find her body and lay it to rest as it should be.

At least now she had real hope…

A Ghostly Diversion

9: Who is she?

Helen heard the car on the drive and knew it was James. Thoroughly annoyed, she waited until she could hear footsteps on the gravel indicating that James was about to reach the door which, with one quick move, she flung open angrily and looked out at him.

"WHERE THE HEL...." She looked at his dishevelled and pathetic figure shivering in the doorway and immediately felt guilty. "What's happened?" She cried and quickly got him inside. Running upstairs, she fetched a set of towels as James began to strip off his drenched clothes and clumsily made his way up to their bathroom.

He sneezed several times in quick succession and knew that he had gone too far this time and she would have to know the truth. Helen continued fussing over him as he undressed, shaking her head, and muttering about him catching his death of cold as she wrapped James in his favourite dressing gown and they both went downstairs to the living room.

"I'll get the kettle on – but what the hell's going on James? Where have you been? I've been worried sick, and you didn't reply to any of my calls!" She said as she headed out into the kitchen shaking her head. James fished out his phone from the dressing gown pocket and realised he must have accidentally switched it to silent mode.

There were around seven missed calls and several texts, not just from Helen but from his boss Mark as well asking where he was and if he was alright. A few moments later she was back whilst the kettle did its duty and she sat down next to him watching him, not knowing whether to be angry or concerned.

"James? What's going on love? You've been strange for some weeks now and I'm... well I'm..." she was struggling to find the right words to convey her true thoughts and feelings, "...to put it bluntly – who is she?" She blurted out with tears welling up in her eyes.

Helen looked down at her feet saddened that she had had to ask the question, but things seemed to have gone too far now.

James looked up at this and he thought she must know – perhaps he did talk in his sleep after all, or Craig had mentioned something to her.

"I didn't realise you knew about her..." he said softly without really thinking about what he was saying, and Helen's eyes widened and started to fill with tears again. He carried on completely oblivious to her reaction. "I suppose Craig must have said something, but I didn't really know how to tell you – it's so strange I'm not even sure I understand or believe what's been happening".

A tear rolled down Helen's soft cheek and she had to check herself as she wasn't sure, but, to her ears, James had just admitted there was indeed another woman. She swallowed hard and faced him as calmly as she could. Something though inside her was puzzled by his words. This wasn't like James at all and what did he mean by not believing it himself?

"I think you owe me an explanation, but for your information Craig has been a loyal friend to you and not told me anything about your fancy bit on the

A Ghostly Diversion

side – it's your own behaviour that's given you away."

Tears once again welled up in her eyes – she had not really expected a confession like this and didn't want to believe that her worst fears were being confirmed.

"So, who is she? – I'd like to get my hands on that bitch and give her what for…" She was now getting her inner strength back, but she suddenly noticed that James was looking at her strangely.

"Err… I've missed something." He muttered as he shook his head from side to side "…what bit on the side?" He asked cautiously somewhat confused by the turn of events. Helen started to get angry and stood up holding one of the cushions to her chest.

"Don't take me for a fool – you can't backtrack on what you've just said you idiot. Go on – what's her NAME?"

James looked blankly up at her, partially amazed at this new aspect of his normally caring wife. He sneezed again and wiped his nose with his handkerchief.

"I don't understand – I don't know her name, she's dead for heaven's sake!"

Helen had been gently swaying back and forth as she tried to calm herself down but now stopped in her tracks and looked at James in shock and disbelief.

"WHAT?" She cried is disbelief and sat down heavily on the sofa. "You've, you've KILLED HER?" She was aghast but incredulous at the same time.

Clearly James was having a breakdown or something, she tried telling herself, but he was now insisting she listen to him and let him tell her everything.

Everything?

What more could there be?

She steeled herself mentally for what she dreaded might be the next confession. Were there others? Helen wasn't sure she could take this apparent turn of events, but she managed to calm down enough to fold her arms across her chest. She turned to face the person she had always thought she could trust implicitly. She sat down facing him and he insisted on holding her hands in his. Reluctantly she let him, ready to pull them away when the pain and hurt got too much, as indeed she expected it to, now that things were coming out in the open.

James drew a deep breath, coughed, then settled down and began to tell her about the cottage, from the first time he'd actually noticed it until Craig and he visited the inn the other week but Helen had begun to shake her head in disbelief.

"No, no, **No!** Lies, all lies, I don't believe I'm hearing this from you. You could have come up with a better excuse. Just tell me **WHO SHE IS?** Then you can piss off back to her place for all I care."

Helen got up angrily and went to the gas fireplace her head down and eyes closed as she struggled with what she'd said to the man she loved, but who had clearly betrayed her. James stood up and tried to hold her shoulders lovingly from behind, but she shrugged him off.

"But sweetheart, this *IS* the truth." He sneezed suddenly. "I find it hard to believe it as well which is why I struggled to tell you. But Craig was right all along – I should have told you earlier."

A Ghostly Diversion

She shook her head and brushed past him into the kitchen and began pushing things around and rearranging things just for the sake of something to take her mind off what was happening. Impulsively she slammed the smallest of their saucepan down hard on the kitchen work top and startled herself with the sheer force of the act.

James stood shocked at events then had a sudden thought. "Wait, I've got something that will show I'm telling the truth."

He rushed out of the room and up the stairs, starting off another coughing and sneezing fit in the process as he went.

"Don't think you can get round me like that either!" She shouted after him and went back into the living room and over to the sofa sitting down heavily. The tears trickled down her face once more as she began to sob, holding her head in her hands.

Within moments, though, she heard James rushing down the stairs and he came into the room with a new round of sneezes and handed her a clear acetate file folder which appeared to have something like pink dust smeared all over a piece of faded newspaper.

She chucked it down to the side on the sofa in disgust, but James picked it up again.

"For heaven's sake, Helen, just LOOK at it will you!" he turned away and looked in the mirror, " I can't believe you see me like that – I would NEVER do anything like that to you – you know me better than that. LOOK AT IT and give me a chance!" He pleaded.

She reluctantly picked the acetate folder up and turned it over, inspecting it, but with little enthusiasm. However, the crumbling remains of the picture caught her eye and she dried them to get a better view.

She stared more closely at the picture and the headline above it, becoming more intrigued, but still the pain in her heart kept reminding her that in her eyes James had confessed to an affair. She put it back down and looked down at her slippers.

James came back over to her and sat down but she shuffled to the side of the sofa, and he shook his head not knowing what more to say. The clock on the mantelpiece suddenly chimed for eleven p.m. and it seemed to stir Helen into a decision, and she got up slowly.

"I need time to think things over. I'm going to bed. ***You*** can have the sofa." And with that she didn't give him chance to appeal to her as she rushed out of the room and James heard her pound her way up the stairs to their bedroom. He looked around and shivered again. Carefully tiptoeing up the stairs he managed to find sheets in the airing cupboard, and he reluctantly went back down and tried to settle on the sofa.

A couple of times during the night he tried to slip into the bedroom hoping against hope that Helen had softened and had realised he was telling the truth. The answer was an emphatic "GO AWAY" and the rest of the night was a sleepless affair of coughing and sneezing fits and a struggle to get comfy on the sofa.

It was a long night indeed.

#

A Ghostly Diversion

Morning dawned too quickly however for James and he felt terrible. His head and body were aching all over and he couldn't stop his fits of sneezing. His throat kept going dry and he couldn't seem to get things into focus properly. He heard sounds upstairs and decided to head on up to the bathroom to get his ablutions done ready for work.

The stairs seemed to take forever and the sounds he had heard were Helen going into the bathroom herself, locking the door behind her. Bleary eyed, he wandered into their bedroom and crashed out on the bed wishing he'd never gone to, indeed never seen, 'Wolds View' cottage at all.

He didn't hear her come into the room and he drifted in and out of what must have been a semi-conscious state. Helen came over dressed still in her lilac dressing gown and sat down next to him. He started to cough and sneeze in fits and starts and she gently ran her hand through his hair. She'd had a lot to think about during the night and the pain was still there, but James was her husband, and it was not like him at all to be ill, or for that matter unfaithful.

She knew in her heart that she had to give him some leeway – perhaps there was something to his story, but for now, she knew he needed her.

Men!

Like children sometimes, she reflected, they always need someone to look after them. They never really left their mother's bosom. She shook her head and struggled to roll James into the bed, covering him with the sheets. Helen felt his forehead and again shook her head. He was in no fit state for work, that was for sure, but it was too early to try to get hold of Mark.

A Ghostly Diversion

Quickly getting dressed she went down into the kitchen, rummaged through their medical cabinet and found the needed items. Taking the medicine upstairs she gently rocked James and he stirred and again started coughing with a rough rasp. She held the plastic mug to his lips, and he drank the mixture down before settling back and drifting off into his own troubled world. She shook her head again with a lost look on her face not quite sure what to do.

Downstairs she again picked up the acetate folder with the newspaper clippings and studied them. She shook her head not knowing what to believe anymore but deep inside she needed to know more. She glanced up at the clock over the fireplace. Nearly 9 a.m. now, she guessed that Mark or at least someone would be at the office by now. She picked up her smart phone and pressed the smart key for James' work.

She'd never actually phoned them at this new place. James had never missed a day off work either at the old place or here, so it felt strange. The inevitable trash music kicked in whilst she waited for someone to pick up. Getting fed up she almost put it down when a female operator came online, and she breathed a sigh of relief.

"Oh yes, hello, my name's Helen Hansone, my husband is James. Hansone, yes that's right" she listened to the lass on the other end who at least knew of James and a brief pang passed through her as she wondered if the operator was her, the *one*, his *bit on the side* - if indeed there was one. Quickly dismissing the thought and thinking on her feet she carried on,

A Ghostly Diversion

"I'm afraid James' car broke down last night on the way home in the rain and he got soaked. Looks like he's gone down with either a bad cold or the start of flu, so he won't be in today. Give Mr Hendriks, James' apologies, hopefully over the weekend he'll pick up and be back in on Monday."

The person on the other end of the line muttered about passing on the message and Helen finished the call and put her phone down on the coffee table.

She deliberated for a moment then went upstairs to see how he was doing and found him sleeping soundly like a baby, snuggled up in the bed cradling her pillow. She smiled briefly and again shook her head and turned her attention to what she needed to do today. Fortunately, it was Friday, she worked only part time in the tourist information shop, Tuesday to Thursdays so today was her day off.

Mid-morning, she picked up the phone again and after a brief hesitation she called her mum, Bridget, over at Woolsthorpe near Grantham in the south of the county. "Hi mum, err, are you able to spare a few minutes for a chat?"

The next half hour saw Helen pour out her troubles whilst trying to defend James and agree with her mother at the same time – despite Bridget wanting Helen to leave him and go and stay with her for a few days. Eventually Helen managed to settle her mum down; she agreed that if anything did come to light and there was indeed another woman, then she would be down as soon as she could. She put the phone down and it immediately buzzed.

It was James' boss, Mark.

"OK so how is the old bugger then?" Mark Hendriks did not stand on ceremonies.

Helen filled him in on James condition but left out the personal side of things and Mark seemed satisfied and wished James well and to be back as soon as possible, noting that it was a rare thing indeed for James to be ill, so he'd let him off this once.

The phone fell silent, and she felt at a loss as to what to do next. Looking out the window it seemed a nice day, the weather front had swept past them and moved across the sea into Belgium apparently. She slipped her boots on and took a slow walk round the garden picking out a weed here and a weed there, all the time mulling over the events of the previous evening. Finally, she headed back indoors only to spot the phone flashing a missed call and she picked it up and clicked call-back.

"Hello?"

It was Craig on the other end, of all people. "Sorry to bother you Mrs Hansone but I just wondered how James was?" She hesitated, not knowing what to tell him or give away what James had tried to tell her last night. Craig seemed to anticipate her thoughts, however. "Has err… has James said anything about 'Wolds View' yet?" Her attention was caught now, and she murmured an affirmative but offered nothing else.

"Ah I'm glad 'bout that I didn't like the idea of me knowing all about the ghost girl and not you. I…" Helen's attention snapped into sharp focus.

"Ghost?" Helen replied and things went quiet on the other end of the line.

A Ghostly Diversion

"Oh err... I think, well...you mean...you don't know about the, err, ghost girl at the cottage?" Helen moved over to the sofa and picked up the clear folder with the clippings in and turned it over in her hand inspecting it with fresh eyes.

"Sorry Craig, I've been a bit distracted with James coming home last night drenched. He told me something last night about this girl, but he was in no fit state and didn't make a lot of sense. Tell me, where is this cottage and girl?" She tilted her head to one side in a thoughtful pose whilst Craig filled her in on the details. "I think I would like to have a look for myself."

"Would you mind if I go with you, I don't want to sound melodramatic but even I find the place spooky despite not having actually seen anything myself. I finish work at 1 p.m. today and if I go without lunch, I could get the bus to Baumber if you could pick me up there?"

She looked at her watch and thought for a moment. Does she trust Craig? Well, why not. She confirmed the arrangements then clicked off. It didn't take long to sort out some soup for James; as she went up the stairs to see how he was, she kept running through what excuse she could use to go out and leave him for a while. Helen heard him coughing and sneezing again and felt a brief pang of guilt for planning on going out whilst he was laid up in bed unwell. The feeling passed though as she remembered what had gone on the previous night and she stiffened her resolve.

James was half awake as she entered the room and he watched her approach and place a tray with a drink and a bowl of soup next to it, not

A Ghostly Diversion

knowing what she would say or whether she finally believed him. His pleading eyes though started to soften her resolve.

"Sweetheart, I need to get some more painkillers and things for the weekend for us as well as clearing my head so I'm popping out for an hour or so over lunch. Will you be all right?" She said softly and James relaxed a little, she seemed to have calmed down now and perhaps had more faith in him.

He nodded and with a rough voice thanked her for the tea and soup, adding he hoped she wouldn't be long as he was missing her already. He knew it sounded lame and so did she, but Helen just smiled then went out of the bedroom into the bathroom and found her scent.

A few squirts here, there, and just a touch of lip gloss, well, she mused, if one can play away then so can the other, ghost or no ghost ...

10: Two can play at that game...

As the car pulled up at the bus stop in Baumber, Helen spotted Craig, recognising him from their brief encounter the previous Saturday. He opened the passenger door and jumped in after spotting the car was the one James normally drove. He said 'hello, nice to meet you' somewhat nervously, noticing a nice aroma wafting in his direction and felt slightly uncomfortable wondering if he was doing the right thing. Then a thought struck him.

"I thought James had trouble with the car last night?"

Helen turned to him and smiled warmly.

"No, that was my excuse to your boss. Something happened to James at the cottage that must have kept him out in the rain for a couple of hours last night. That's how he's caught his death of cold." She turned and looked straight at Craig, "So now you tell me all you know about this girl and this here cottage, and *I MEAN EVERYTHING*."

Craig felt uncomfortable again as he had the feeling, she hadn't been told very much at all – just how much *had* James told her, he wondered? He filled her in with what he knew whilst giving directions to where they needed to be and within a quarter of an hour, they pulled up outside 'Wolds View'. Helen peered through the windscreen and examined the cottage.

"Pretty desolate, isn't it? So, you don't know who owns the place? Quite stupid of you both to have gone inside someone else's property, you know. " she said, slightly more sharply than she'd really intended. Craig couldn't help but nod in agreement, got out, and instinctively went round and opened her door for her. Helen smiled inwardly at this gentlemanly behaviour and swung her legs to get out, accidentally catching her skirt and partially exposing her upper thigh. She quickly got out and straightened it as Craig blushed and turned away pretending not to notice but he felt a mix of emotions come over him.

Helen knew she was trying to be something she wasn't and now she too felt a little embarrassed at what she was doing. She quietly apologised, straightened her skirt once again and shut the car door. They both looked at the building, but nothing stirred and for a short embarrassing moment there was silence between them.

Craig motioned to her and walked forward so Helen followed as they walked round to the back entrance and stepped inside. It was cold, but Craig felt nothing unusual as they explored the cottage from top to bottom. Upstairs he showed Helen the crumbling plaster and found some more wallpaper peeling away exposing additional clippings, so they carefully removed them to take away. Several times Craig felt as though they were being watched but there was no sign of the 'ghostly girl'. After twenty minutes they headed downstairs, out the back door and walked back around the cottage to the car.

"Perhaps James is a sort of catalyst?" Craig ventured and he could tell Helen was in deep thought. So much so that they didn't notice the dark green Range Rover draw up next to the car and it startled them. Craig recognized the somewhat grizzled looking man behind the wheel. It was the same Range Rover that had pulled over when James

A Ghostly Diversion

had thought he'd run the girl over the other week when it was misty, and they were late home from work.

"Strange for a courting couple to be wandering about, especially that place of all places." He said and Helen looked aghast as she realised what the stranger had implied.

She glanced quickly at Craig.

"Oh no, we're just friends actually, my husband err, well he claims to have seen a ghost here…" she tailed off realising she may be digging an even bigger hole for the two of them.

The driver looked at Helen then at Craig, back to Helen and his gaze settled back on Craig again.

"You're the bloke that was with the other chap that looked as if he'd seen a ghost the other week, aren't you?" Craig nodded and the driver looked back at Helen and gave her the once over, raised his eyebrows at her figure and smiled. "Thought I recognised the car. Guess the other chap's your hubby then?" Helen nodded but didn't appreciate the way he had looked at her and so took the initiative.

"Is it true then? There is a ghost of a girl here?" The driver looked at her and seemed to be making a decision. He got out, walked over to them, and stood looking at the cottage with his hands on his hips contemplating what to say as he shook his head.

"It sounds as if your husband has seen her all right. All I can tell you is that more'n fifty years ago a young couple with a daughter lived here in this cottage. But the young lass disappeared and has never been found. I guess she's still on the Police's missing persons list. Most of the locals ended up thinking she must be dead, but the family clung to hope. Anyhow her father died 'bout a year after and her mother moved away; nobody's seen sight nor sound of the mother since.

The place was left empty but when the estate changed hands during the eighties the new owners did a quick revamp and let it out. A young couple stayed, 'bout a year I guess, then left hurriedly saying the place was haunted by a girl and they too have not been seen here since. Nobody'll go near the place now - that's why it's got into such a state. Shame really as it is solidly built and would make a fine home.

That's all I know. Then I saw your husband and this fella parked here one night in the mist, must be a week or two ago now." He looked Craig up and down, "Must admit I thought you were a gay couple but seems like I was wrong."

Craig stepped back somewhat shocked whilst Helen chuckled a little. "*and* your hubby didn't half look white! I reckon he must have seen her, what you say mate?" He turned to Craig who nodded in agreement.

"James thought he'd run over a young girl who suddenly appeared out of the mist but I myself didn't see anything. When we came back a few days later during the daytime I would say the place went exceedingly cold and James did say she had appeared to him again."

The driver looked at them soberly and grimaced at the knowledge Craig and the other chap had been snooping around the cottage without permission.

"Well for a start you were trespassing, but under the circumstances I'll let it pass. Personally, I've never believed in all that claptrap about ghosts, but folks round here don't go near the place and tend to get a bit uppity if you start asking too many questions. I gather you", He pointed directly at Craig, "were doing that the other week at the inn. I'd stay away if I were you."

He turned to Helen.

"And tell that husband of yours as well. I'm sure you've got plenty more things to do than run around after things that don't exist! I manage the estate around here and that includes the cottage, so I'll be on the lookout for any trespassers yer mind."

He turned away then stopped and looked back at them as if about to say something else, but he shook his head instead. "Remember, *no* trespassing!" He walked round the Range Rover, quickly got in and headed off in the direction of Grasceby.

Helen looked quietly at the ground and shuffled her feet looking thoughtful and upset.

"I didn't believe him Craig. He came home in a hell of a state last night and I accused him of betraying me and having another woman." A tear appeared in her eyes and Craig put his arm around her waist to sooth her.

"Come on" he said "I've not actually seen anything but it is pretty spooky in there when he's with me so I think he must be some sort of conduit for whatever it is. You weren't to know. Must have seemed kind of strange to you these last few weeks. I did tell him to tell you all about it, but I guess it's

A Ghostly Diversion

such a strange story I still find it hard to believe even now."

As he said this, he could smell the scent Helen had put on and for a moment he felt something stir and flutter inside. She was an older woman but extremely attractive and he could see what James must see in her. He switched off the feelings, annoyed with himself. They let go of each other and she went round to the driver's side.

"I'm sorry if I embarrassed you Craig, I didn't mean to. Come on, I'd better get back to him and see how he is. I'll drop you off home and when I know more about what happened last night in the rain, I'll get him to call you, or ..." She hesitated briefly, "... I will." He nodded at her, they smiled at each other, got in the car, and set off towards Grasceby.

#

She watched them go and felt, in her ghostly way, very strange. She didn't hear their conversation outside but realised from the discussions in the cottage between Craig and the woman called Helen that she was James' wife, and he was not well. She had decided to remain in the background and not make herself visible to either of them as she was wary of their reaction to her, but it seemed like her fear over James last night could come true.

'Please let him be all right God', she prayed and hoped that he would be back on his feet quickly. She wondered what she could do if, or when, he came back to her and how she could let him know the circumstances of her death.

A Ghostly Diversion

She settled once more onto her ghostly bed and looked out the window to the blue sky beyond and sighed, gently shaking her head.

11: Turning detective…

"How are you feeling, my love?"

Helen leaned over and spoke gently to him. The words were like music to his ears and her tone was totally different now. She explained to James what she had been up to and reminded him that she hadn't waited to tell him, a strong hint he should never fail to do likewise in the future. It was still a little difficult for Helen, but at least a ghost was better than another woman and for that she was grateful, even if it did make her come out in goose bumps at the thought of it.

As James improved over the weekend, he explained what had happened the other night in the rain and her interest and curiosity grew.

"What do you make of it, then?" she asked as she brought him a coffee on Sunday morning, and he indicated he wanted to get up out of bed.

"I don't know for sure but to me I think she is somehow buried in the side of a ditch, either that or it's where she died, and she's buried somewhere else. You say the guy confirmed there was a girl then?" She sat on her side of the bed, nodded and he continued.

"My guess is that she's dead and she never ran away, she was killed. Question is – who killed her and how come they seem to have got away with it for so long?"

He looked down into his half-drunk coffee. "Wonder where we could find out more?" He looked up at her and as always Helen had an answer.

A Ghostly Diversion

"Call yourself a computer expert? Well, I don't know, what are you like? If you don't know the answer to that then heaven helps us." She laughed at him, and he threw her pillow at her which she skilfully dodged, caught and threw back at him scoring a bullseye.

"Hey - I build them, I service them, I sift through data, but I'm no detective you know!" Helen looked at him and shrugged.

"Webnet, local archives - perhaps the library. We'd need to look for newspaper clippings – oh!" she suddenly remembered the new set of clippings she and Craig had found on their trip to 'Wolds View' and dashed out of the bedroom and downstairs.

Moments later, and a little out of breath, she came back and sat at the edge of the bed next to James, brushing her tousled hair out of her eyes. She handed him a large envelope and inside was a hand sized fragment of newspaper. James looked at it and began reading aloud.

"*...lice*, I think that must be *Police, confirmed today that both suspects had been released after intensive questioning and were no longer wanted in the case of the disappearance of Jennifer Anne Portisham (16) of Wolds View Cottage, Grasceby. It has been two weeks since she was last seen and despite an exte…*"

Part of the clipping was missing so he skipped to where it remained and was readable. "*nd local residents, there are no clues as to her whereabouts. The family confirmed that there seemed to be no reason for her to run off and that she had been planning to meet up with her boyfriend on the day she dis….*"

The rest was missing. James looked up at Helen. "Jennifer Portisham. So that's who she is …"

he corrected himself, "was." He sniffed and then tried to downplay it - he was beginning to feel more like himself now and was eager to find out who this Jennifer was. "If I wrap up warm, are you going to let me get up and have a search on the web?"

He looked pleadingly at Helen, and she could see it would be no good telling him not to, so she nodded her approval but made a point of insisting that if he felt unwell he was to go back to bed.

"OK. Mark won't be very happy with you if you're not back to work as soon as you can! Give me a shout if you find anything interesting, I'm going to sort out what we're having for lunch." She got up and left the room and it didn't take James long to be up and accessing the web via his smart tablet.

"Portisham, Portisham." He kept repeating to himself as he typed the name into the search engine and waited – a split second – there was thousands of references. And all of them, it seemed, concerned the village of Portesham in Dorset. James had not realised it was also a place but even when he tried to refine the search it either came back with nothing or he ended up again with lots of information on everything you needed to know about Portesham village and the surrounding countryside.

He tried a different tack. Typing 'Lincolnshire newspapers' he found several with their own web sites and saved the search page so he could carry on after lunch as he heard Helen calling up to him.

#

A Ghostly Diversion

Lunch over, James headed straight back upstairs and began searching the newspaper sites. A couple of hours later Helen came into the room with a coffee for him.

"Any luck?" She asked and James shook his head. Although virtually all the local newspapers nowadays had web sites with an archive section there were tens of thousands of scanned newspapers and it seemed not all were fully searchable yet.

"Try Lincoln Archives, I'd make a bet that they would have put some of their resources up online by now." Helen offered as she headed back out of the door to go downstairs. James fed the info into the search site, and it threw up hundreds of links. He began looking down them to see if any would take him to something of use in his search.

A few minutes rolled by but then he hit a small jackpot. One of the links referred to a "missing persons web site" – something neither of them had thought of and he clicked on it.

Another twenty minutes slipped by, and James was beginning to tire, there were sadly thousands upon thousands of people missing, not just the UK, but all over the world. The on-site search engine had thrown up nothing on Jennifer Portisham, indeed nothing except lots of references to 'Jennifer' this, that and the other. He sighed and clicked the next link and scanned the page quickly and clicked for the last page…

…and backed up again to the one he'd just left. He hadn't quite got to the bottom of the page when he clicked to move on, but his eye had caught something.

A Ghostly Diversion

There she was!

He read then re-read the short entry.

Jenny Portisham Aged 16Y 5M 12D

Full name: Jennifer Anne Portisham

Born: November 20th 1943

Last known Address: 'Wolds View' Cottage, Grasceby, Lincolnshire.

Missing since: Saturday April 9th 1960

Possible reason: Not known/runaway?

Last update: Feb 18th 2002 (Paper records scanned and transferred to digital format).

That was it.

"Jenny", mused James, that's why he hadn't found her quicker, "never gave it a thought. A bit sloppy really when the main reference should have been her full name in the first place." He sighed, then he heard Helen coming up the stairs. She popped her head round the corner of the door on hearing him talking to himself.

"Anything?" He shook his head and shrugged his shoulders in a funny way.

"Well sort of, it's a bit short and sweet, take a look." He wirelessly transferred the output to their wall display as it changed from a stunning snowy alpine view to the info he'd found. Helen frowned as she quickly took in the info and turned back to him.

"How about us going to the library and perhaps the Lincolnshire Archives? They're bound to have copies of the original newspapers that carried the story." He nodded his head in agreement and shut down the wall display.

"I'm half day at work on Tuesday" he said "so perhaps we can do it then? That's if Mark doesn't make me stay extra for missing a day off work." He quickly checked the archives web site and looked up the opening and closing times to confirm they could go then. Satisfied he had got as much as he could from the web, James followed Helen downstairs ready for dinner, he'd got quite hungry after all that research.

#

Knowing what Mark was like, James was pleased to see that his boss did have a human side to him as he didn't want James to make up the lost day. As long as his 'top bloke' was well and fit to work he was just happy to have him back. James knew he was quite lucky having such a good boss, not every company was like that, he reflected. Still, they had also been friends for what felt like all of eternity, since Uni, in fact so he guess that must have counted for something.

Tuesday quickly came and James and Helen called in at Lincoln Archives. It took, it seemed, forever for them to complete the forms and get their photos taken for their cards but finally they entered the main room ready to start their search. The assistant had been most helpful and guided then to the vast section covering archived newspapers and indeed anything that might help, including police reports from the era that had been made public in the hope of finding more information on the missing Jennifer.

Helen thanked the courteous assistant again and headed over to the appropriate section to begin looking along the various references to the local newspapers. It seemed a thankless task at first, as

A Ghostly Diversion

there seemed to be so much to look through, but gradually she seemed to be down to just a few copies on a quaint old microfiche set in one corner of the large room. She was surprised at the archaic equipment but then it would be a horrendous job putting all that data into a format suitable for a computer. Perhaps James could take a look at it for them, she wondered idly.

Meanwhile he was over the other side of the room looking at the police records when Helen motioned for him to come over to her.

"Hey - take a look at this" she said in a hushed tone so as not to disturb several other people in the room, two of which turned and gave them a stern look. She indicated at the microfiche. James looked at the old technology bemused but then the writing caught his attention.

'A young couple today fled a Lincolnshire cottage after claiming it was haunted by a ghost. Stephen and Patricia Ollerden had rented 'Wolds View' cottage on the outskirts of the tiny village of Grasceby near Horncastle for just over a year.

Shortly after moving in, they began to notice a cold feeling in the upstairs rooms especially the smaller of the two bedrooms. On at least five occasions, explained Mr Ollerden, a ghost of a young girl seemed to drift from one room to the other and back before vanishing and on at least one occasion his wife, Patricia, had seen the apparition in the garden at the front of the property.

They had complained to the landlord, but he shrugged it off as an excuse to get out of paying their monthly rent, however they had discovered from the local villagers that a young girl had disappeared

A Ghostly Diversion

around twenty years previously and her whereabouts were not known. Our reporter can confirm that a Jennifer Portisham had indeed gone missing from the property and to this day her whereabouts have not been established. A Police spokesman, Detective Inspector Michael Freshman, confirmed that a Jennifer Anne Portisham had gone missing on April 9th 1960 and that the case had gone cold.

Despite extensive enquiries the police spokesman stated there was no evidence of foul play and that her parents and boyfriend had been cleared of suspicion and were not considered suspects. However, the case continues to baffle investigators. Although the 'ghost' sightings were unusual they could not be considered firm evidence of foul play. The case remains open but currently is not considered a high priority unless firm and tangible evidence appears that can help with enquiries. The assistant to Grasceby Manor estate, a Mr Frank Colby, refused to speculate either on the claimed ghost or the previous occupants and their daughter's disappearance.'

James looked at Helen.

"Wow - if I lived there, I'd want to move out as well!" he said. "So, we could do with talking to the Manor's assistant, Mr Colby."

Helen looked puzzled though and she frowned as she looked through the small box of microfiches quickly.

"I don't think that's going to be possible love, he died about three years ago. I came across that name a moment ago when I was looking through some obituaries earlier and spotted his link with the cottage. It's interesting that I can't seem to find anyone by the surname of Portisham at all listed anywhere. The family must have moved out of the county after Jenny disappeared".

James looked thoughtful then had an idea.

"Perhaps if we can find the investigating officer at the time and talk to him then we might find out more? That Detective perhaps?" Helen nodded and James went back to searching the police records.

An hour later and at last James came across the right series of reports giving him the name of the officer in charge of the original investigation; however, it wasn't Detective Inspector Mike Freshman but another Detective by the name of Heath.

Helen suddenly came over and grabbed James by the arm. "Look at this, I've found a brief report in the local newspaper for about a year after Jenny's disappearance. It's another obituary - Mr Jack Portisham. It says that Mr Jack Frederick Portisham, aged 38, whose daughter Jenny vanished over a year ago, died suddenly in the night. His wife believes it was due to a broken heart as he adored his daughter and struggled to cope with her disappearance. A post-mortem concluded that Mr Portisham did indeed die of heart failure but that unbeknownst to him, his family or their GP, he appeared to have had a rare but serious congenital heart condition."

Helen looked at James and raised her eyebrows then turned back to the document. "Wow - listen to this, 'Mr Portisham is survived by his wife Barbara, 36 who was with child, approximately seven months into the pregnancy'."

A Ghostly Diversion

"How sad" said James looking over her shoulder "Don't you think that's really sad - daughter vanishes, father dies, and the poor mum has a baby on the way to cope with as well - talk about a bad run of luck."

Helen nodded in agreement.

"What's more there is another reference to that family having experienced tragedy in the past but when I tried to look it up, I couldn't find anything, as if there were sections missing in the archives. I'll just ask at the desk, wait here."

Helen didn't take long to come back but now had sheaves of paper, copies to take away with them when they'd finished. At least now they had something more to go on even if it didn't explain what happened to Jennifer.

"Well, what about the missing sections?" James quietly asked. "Seems there was a fire, and some records were lost hence there are gaps in the older records. Pity as I wonder what other tragedy the Portishams had gone through earlier?"

"Probably never know. Oh well, home now and see what we can make of what we have got." He replied as they headed out of the door.

12: The 'Freshman' investigation…

The Policeman on duty did not look particularly impressed with James. He looked him up and down and then took a deep breath. "So, sir, let me understand you. You've seen the ghost of a girl that vanished at least fifty years ago, and she's told you she was murdered and didn't run away. You want to talk to the investigating officer at the time and help with the investigation. Would you say that's a fair summary sir?"

James looked at him and inside his stomach sank a little as, put in that way, even he thought his story now sounded silly. He shuffled on his feet nervously and tried to maintain a serious tone.

"Err, well that's about right although Jenny didn't actually talk to me and I'm not sure she was murdered actually but that's what I'm trying to get to the bottom of. So, if I could …"

He could see the Policeman was looking at him in a slightly incredulous manner, but James put on his serious face. "I'm sure officer that it does sound a bit far-fetched but if I could talk to Det Insp Heath or Detective Inspector Freshman then they might be able to help me. Could you get them for me please?"

The officer looked at James and slightly shook his head and moved his sheaf of papers to one side.

"Sir, I've been here now for about eleven years, and I don't recall either of those names and if I'm honest I've never heard anything like this before. However, just humour me and I'll check with Jerry to

A Ghostly Diversion

see if there was a Heath or Freshman here all that time ago."

The officer slipped through a back door and was gone for at least ten minutes whilst James wandered round the reception looking at various posters in an attempt to keep himself from giving up in despair. An attractive red-haired woman with an air of importance entered the station and swiped her pass card to allow her into the back area behind the desk. She gave James a quick glance, smiled faintly and nodded at him, then she stopped to pick up some papers, scanning them quickly with her hazel eyes just as the constable came back.

"Fletcher, are these the very latest lab results on that drug raid we did last week in Bardney?"

Constable Fletcher nodded.

"I believe so ma'am." She turned, looked James up and down again acknowledged his presence with another brief nod and the faintest hint of a smile, then took the papers into a back room without further comment. Constable Fletcher visibly relaxed and turned to see James was now looking out the window across the street.

A cough brought James promptly back to the desk.

"Well to be fair, there was indeed both officers stationed here and yes they did deal with the occasional missing persons case for the county. Det Insp Gerald Heath passed away some years ago, but his successor was Det Insp Freshman. However, he moved to another force a couple of years before I arrived here. As far as my colleague is aware the Inspector retired about three years ago but has returned to Lincolnshire."

James brightened up at this last piece of information.

"Can I have his mobile number then or his address, this is great news - thanks. "

The officer frowned at him though.

"Sorry sir, can't give out that sort of personal information, data protection act and all that, however if you'd like to leave me your contact details then I will see if I can get hold of him for you and then it's up to him if he calls you. That's the best I can do for you."

James jotted down his details and thanked the officer for his help. The visit had not been a total waste after all but now he could only wait and hope that this retired Detective Inspector would indeed get in touch.

#

Three weeks passed by and with no contact James and Helen were coming to realise they were at a dead end. Work was now getting busy for James whilst Helen herself had plenty to do as she'd joined the local ladies' group amongst other local social projects. In talking to her newfound friends in the group she'd discovered precious little to add to what they already knew. Even the eldest lady in the group, ninety-four-year-old Rose, seemed to know little about the Portishams of the nineteen fifties and in particular April 1960 as she'd come to the county from Lancashire in the late nineteen sixties. True to form she did also enjoy reminding everyone how old she was.

A Ghostly Diversion

Whilst he was seated at the table with his tablet computer, coffee in hand, James' smart phone chirped to say he had a call and as he looked down at the display he noted it was his boss, Mark. Odd, he thought, he was having a few days off and didn't really expect there to be any reason for Mark to call him. He picked up the call.

"Hi Mark, what gives?"

"Who's been a naughty boy then? Sorry James - no worries, but we have had a chap by the name of Mike Freshman call in and ask for you."

James sat bolt upright - his attention well and truly grabbed.

"And...?" Was all he could ask.

"Oh, he just asked if you were about, and I gave him your details - so he's not been in touch then?"

"No - did he call in today then?"

"Yes, about a couple of hours ago. Anyhow he didn't leave any details except to say he used to be in Lincolnshire Police stationed at Horncastle, but I thought I'd just let you know".

James thanked Mark and closed the link as he filled Helen in with the news. 'Funny that, he hadn't given his work details to the officer at the police station so why did Mike Freshman turn up there and how would he know where to go?' He thought out loud.

Helen just shrugged.

"Well, he is or was a detective after all!" She noted and they both smiled at the idea of James being important enough to be investigated just because he'd asked about a ghost.

A Ghostly Diversion

\#

The next evening, they had just finished dinner and cleared everything away when the doorbell chimed. *And* for a second time, just as James got to it, he hated people doing that! Why not just press the bell once and give it a few minutes he thought as he approached the door wondering if it was a cold caller. 'Blooming gas and electricity people I bet' he thought as he reached, then opened the door. Standing in the front porch was a grey haired, slightly balding, gentleman with an air of grace about his person.

"James Hansone?"

"Err - yes, yes," James looked at the gentleman and a thought occurred to him as he tilted his head, "Mike Freshman?" He tentatively asked. The gentleman smiled and nodded; James motioned eagerly for him to come in. "Thanks for calling by, can I take your coat?"

"As long as you give it back, I can tell you that you won't get much for it on an online auction site that's for sure!" Mike quipped and smiled as they went into the living room just as Helen also came in and they exchanged greetings.

"Can I offer you a drink?" She asked.

"That would be very kind of you, would you have Earl Grey tea by any chance?" She nodded and went off into the kitchen as Mike turned to James.

"So, you're interested in the Portisham case I gather, something about ghosts, as I understand it?" Mike said the last bit with his eyebrows raised and

A Ghostly Diversion

James smiled slightly nervously and glanced at Helen for reassurance.

"Well, yes, you could say that... although I've only seen Jenny - are there others?". Mike looked over at them as he sat down.

"If you believe in such things then it has to be said that most of the reports, I ever came across only mentioned a young girl, but there is at least one account of possibly her father as well not long after he died. May I ask why it is you are so interested in Jenny's disappearance? It's a very old case and I know with the many detective programmes on TV everyone now thinks they can solve any crime under the sun!"

James grimaced at that as he did enjoy the crime dramas but decided to soldier on and over the next half hour poured out all he knew and had experienced over the last few months as they both supped at their drinks Helen had brought for them.

Finally, Mike straightened in his seat. "Well, that's certainly *'interesting'* to say the least." He seemed to be making a point by emphasising the word 'interesting'. He paused for a few moments and appeared to be digesting the story. "Technically the case is still open, but nobody has taken any interest in almost thirty years now. My biggest problem at the time was that the most 'obvious' possibility involved the boyfriend, Richard Dreyer.

Unfortunately, he seemed to have a cast iron alibi for the time and day that Jenny vanished. The case was unusual as the family were well respected and there were no suspicious circumstances as she had apparently been a very happy and talented

A Ghostly Diversion

teenager. Richard, her boyfriend, always appeared as distraught as the family and there was no rhyme or reason for her to disappear.

The parents contacted the police after Jenny had not been seen for a day which wasn't that odd at the time. She was listed as a missing person and the force did a thorough search of the area, with the help of the local villagers, but eventually it was concluded that for some unknown reason she had run away. Although both Jack and Richard had naturally been suspects they had been cleared by us as there was simply no evidence of foul play. No sign of a struggle, the cottage was as tidy as her mum had left it that day - there was just nothing to go on.

The sad thing was that a year or so later Jack was so distraught about the disappearance of his 'little poppet' as he called her, that gradually he just began to fall apart as the months wore on. Nearly a year later he died, some say of a broken heart and the wife, Barbara, decided to move away to start over again just before the birth of their second child.

Det Insp Heath oversaw the investigation at the time and never ever heard from Mrs Portisham again and there are no more records so as you've gathered the trail went cold. I was a newbie just starting out but did some of the main interviews twenty years later when the young couple renting 'Wolds View' fled the cottage.

Something really spooked them. Apparently, both in the cottage and in the nearby woods. One was possibly young Jenny whilst the other may have been a prank by locals as it was a gentleman looking like a Frenchman from a few hundred years ago." He looked deep in thought for a moment, "But in the real world we need hard facts and evidence, not ghosts."

James looked at Helen and back to Mike.

"So, tell me what's your gut instinct now?" asked James.

Mike looked down at his feet and then squarely into James's eyes.

"I don't believe in ghosts myself sir and although you've made an interesting case about her being murdered there really is no evidence so I can't see the local constabulary looking into it again. Richard has gone on to becoming a fairly successful businessman dealing in antiques, a local speciality for Horncastle as you may have noticed from the town signs. Since the other couple fled the cottage, it's been both unsalable and unrentable so there's no wonder it's abandoned and becoming derelict.

I have to say though that you weren't really in the right to go snooping round it." James briefly looked alarmed, but Mike quickly carried on "But rest assured I'm not bothered and not going to report you." He smiled and went to get up but sat down again. "IF you do come across anything else though then here's my contact details as I'd like to think you're wrong and Jenny is somewhere out there living a happy life."

He got up and headed for the door. James shook his hand.

"Thanks for getting in touch Mike and trust me if we come across anything then you'll be the first to know." Mike nodded and smiled at Helen and James as he left, and they both walked back into the lounge to digest what they'd heard that evening.

A Ghostly Diversion

#

As he stepped into his car Mike shook his head. Something was nagging at him from a distant memory that James' account had triggered but for the life of him he couldn't pin it down.

He started his car and drove off troubled by the feeling he was missing something …

13: The second walk…

Despite several trips to the cottage over the following weeks James did not see Jenny again and he began to wonder what had changed to stop her appearing to him. However, he suddenly realised that every time he had visited the cottage either Helen or Craig was with him, and he began to wonder if they were the reason for her not showing.

Helen was not so sure but didn't argue when he said he was going back to 'Wolds View' on his own that afternoon. He'd even found a place to park up away from the cottage, so it didn't attract attention as previously he'd always parked up outside on the verge and in plain view. He was especially keen on not encountering the estate manager who'd given Helen and Craig a so-called friendly warning to stay away.

Twenty minutes later he'd parked up and walked along the lane until once again he reached the clearing where the cottage stood back from the road.

"It really would make a good property done up." He said to himself as he went round the back and in through the still jammed door. He was so tempted to push it fully open but knew that it would tip off the estate manager that someone was snooping around again.

Upstairs all was quiet with no sign of Jenny and after ten minutes James began to wonder what he needed to do for her to appear.

A Ghostly Diversion

Finally, as dusk fell, she appeared in the corner of the smaller bedroom but oddly this time she seemed to be oblivious to James. Once again, she got up from what seemed like an imaginary bed, looked out her window then appeared to get excited and he followed her as she headed downstairs, apparently as happy as a lamb. This time she appeared to greet someone at the door, hug them, then did something with her hands but he couldn't figure out what as she had her back to him.

She seemed to lean forward as if kissing someone, then held an invisible hand and went out the doorway. Only to come back in and appear to write a note and pin it to the outside of the back door but, try as he might, James couldn't see anything of it. Jenny turned and for a split-second James thought she was staring at him, but she smiled and grabbed something from off the mantelpiece and walked back outside.

Keeping a respectful distance James followed her as she walked along the garden path until she reached, then followed, the road to the left. She seemed to be acting playful with someone. Suddenly she looked as if she was being pulled into the hedge and James's heart skipped a beat as he thought this was it - the moment of truth, but after a short while she re-emerged and carried on walking on the roadside.

Suddenly it hit James that she was now doing the same route as a few weeks earlier when he'd got wet through. Sure enough, a little further on she turned left into the thin wood.

A Ghostly Diversion

It then emerged into the field the other side following what appeared to be a typical animal path, probably a fox or badger route cutting across the field.

James followed but kept a discreet distance behind Jenny. She seemed to be playing tag with someone as she approached what he knew to be the drainage ditch and small bridge across it. Gradually he became aware that there was more detail in what she was appearing to re-enact as Jenny seemed pleased and skipped across the invisible bridge and looked back, presumably James thought, to the person she was with, perhaps her boyfriend he wondered.

He got the impression that they embraced and then Jenny appeared to grab at something low down then rush off along the ditch bank. As she did so it was clear they were fooling around as only lovers do as they frolicked along the bank. She seemed to be lovingly punching the other invisible person and teasing them and in retaliation she looked as if they then got her in a headlock position rubbing her hair whilst being close to the edge of the ditch.

Things suddenly happened so quickly that James could barely keep up let alone believe what he saw. Jenny was still smiling playfully even in the so-called headlock - it was clear at that moment it was only a bit of fun.

Suddenly she lost her footing and she slipped down the edge of the drainage ditch twisting whilst still in the headlock position as she did so.

A Ghostly Diversion

It was all over so quickly that James had to blink to take in what he thought he was seeing. Jenny's ghostlike body appeared to twitch and spasm near the bottom of the ditch and for all intents and purposes it looked as if someone was trying to help - but in vain.

The twitching and jerking slowed to a stop as she went limp in what James assumed were her boyfriend's arms. For several long moments the 'lifeless' ghost appeared to be gently rocked back and forth before suddenly being picked up. Her body appeared to be turned one way then the other before being carried back up the side of the ditch and away across the short stretch of field and towards the woods.

Shocked, James felt as if he was going to be sick and stood slightly swaying as his stomach settled down.

He suddenly came out of shock and quickly scrambled down into, then up, the other side of the ditch just in time to see Jenny's ghostly body disappear into the woods and he hurried to catch up. It was getting darker as he brushed back scrub to make a way through into the woods, but it was clear that he'd lost her.

For several long minutes James stood transfixed until he finally shook his head, turned, and headed back to the road to find his car.

"By heck, Helen and Craig are NOT going to believe this" he muttered to himself as he got into the car and set off for home.

#

A Ghostly Diversion

"Bloody Hell!" exclaimed Helen and Craig when James had finished recounting what had happened. He wasn't at all fazed that Craig seemed to be spending more time round at their place.

After all Craig had been the first-person James had told only the other month, so it was good that he
was still taking an interest.

"It has to have been an accident and the only logical thing to explain why Jenny went willingly is that it was her boyfriend - that Richard lad." He said thoughtfully.

"Didn't Mike say the boyfriend was now a successful antiques dealer in Horncastle?" Offered Helen and James nodded.

"But do we let sleeping dogs lie?" Interjected Craig, "Is it worth ruining the reputation of a well-known local businessman for something that happened so long ago? You can't really prove anything, and you'd get laughed at by everyone. You said yourself the local Police were somewhat bemused with how you were supposed to know what happened to her - through her ghost…"

James looked at his muddy shoes and realised he'd trailed the mud across the carpet. By looking down he automatically alerted Helen who looked at the mess and raised an eyebrow at him as much to say, 'you're going to clean that up!' He nodded to her and she smiled back but then smiled at Craig, James noticed it but didn't question her, they were after all sharing a strange sort of adventure together.

A Ghostly Diversion

Still, that was nothing compared with the possibility that he might be able to solve Jenny's disappearance and, he hoped, help her find the peace she deserved.

"I wonder if I should contact Mike - you know the retired detective. He did seem intrigued as I was able to tell him things that wouldn't have come out in the original investigation. I'll drop him a line and see if he'll meet up again. Anyhow it's getting late, guess you'll need a lift home Craig?"

Craig went to answer, however Helen butted in. "Actually, Craig's got some info at his place that might help me - I'm looking into his family tree so if you like I can drop him home and I can pick up the files to bring back - that OK darling?" She aimed a loving smile at James, and he shrugged.

"Yep - see you in the morning at work then Craig." Craig and Helen got up and James brushed past Helen to go into the kitchen. The unmistakable aroma of her favourite scent tickled his nose and he paused and turned to her.

"You smell nice love, special occasion?" Helen seemed to briefly freeze, then quickly regained her composure.

"Oh, I just fancied dabbing a bit on just to freshen up after I got in from work."

James smiled and lightly kissed her on the cheek.

"It is nice. See you later then, don't be too late."

Craig stepped forward and helped her on with her coat, much to Helen's pleasure, before they slipped out the door. James smiled to himself pleased that Helen had got to know Craig better and so adding to their ever-growing circle of friends.

But a tiny part of his mind knew that things were not quite as they seemed, but he dismissed the thought just as quickly as it had formed.

#

For the first time in a very long time, Jenny knew she now had real hope. James had followed her as she had fully re-enacted what had happened all those years ago. The only downside was that he had not followed her into the woods. But surely now it was only a matter of time and she looked out from her bedroom window with a renewed sense of hope.

14: I may be retired, but...

James smiled as he stepped through the door of the inn to see the retired detective sitting at a table near the bar.

"Mike, really glad you came - thought after last time you'd probably blacklist me and ignore my calls!"

Mike smiled and looked slightly up to the, admittedly, low ceiling.

"That did cross my mind." He smiled though and continued. "What will you have then - mind what you say as I know you're driving and once a police officer, always a police officer." he chuckled.

"Ok, best make it an orange juice then." With that Mike nodded to Marcus at the bar and James joined him at the table.

"So, let me guess - you've been trespassing again and seen her ghost as well to boot?" Mike enquired.

James slightly lowered his head.

"Don't put it like that, sounds awful!" He replied but then carried on. "Well, yes, it happened almost identically to the last time but this time there was more. " He went on to explain what he'd seen the other evening. As he finished Marcus brought the orange juice over and leaned down and whispered into James' ear.

"So, not an estate agent after all, on the lookout for new properties, eh? Just so you know you seem to be getting a bit of a wacko reputation in these parts, ghosts an all. Just telling you for your own good. Get my drift?" He stood back up. "That'll be £2, thanks." Mike cocked an eye at Marcus and indicated to put it on his tab, Marcus smiled at him and nodded before turning away back to the bar.

"Don't mind Marcus, he's been here as long as I have and we take time to accept newbies into the area, especially from the south. You come across as a good bloke James and for what it's worth you do seem convinced of what you've seen.

Just so as you don't think you're mad, Marcus has also seen her, once. Shit scared he was an' all as he was in his twenties and cycling past the house. Told me about it a few years back in, let's say, a weak moment, in other words after a few too many! His description of her is pretty much identical to yours, blue top, long summery looking skirt. And that's why I'm interested. You are the *only* person to confirm *exactly* what Marcus saw. Trouble is, it's at odds with what her mother says Jenny was wearing the last time she saw her alive. Now that does intrigue me as, to my knowledge, you had not met Marcus until the other day, and he's already confirmed neither of you mentioned Jenny to the other or what she was wearing. So how come you both can describe her exactly like that if you haven't seen something like her ghost?"

James shrugged and looked at Mike, his gaze drifted across the room to Marcus and back to the retired policeman.

"At least it's not just me then! Listen, I was just as sceptical - indeed I'm a practical person, a bit of a scientist at heart, I've got a degree in Computer engineering, so this has been a shock to me. I didn't ask for any of this to happen and I spend plenty of time wondering if I should see a psychiatrist. But in

A Ghostly Diversion

the end, being of a scientific type I need to follow this through and find out if what I've seen has any basis in reality. Or is it just something my mind conjured up when I was under a bit of work-related strain?

All I ask is for you to just go along with me for a bit longer. If it turns out I'm going nuts, then I apologise for taking up your time."

Mike looked across the table and then seemed to look past James towards the back of the room. He leaned forward and began talking in a hushed voice.

"Don't turn round now but the chap on his own at the back is *Richard Dreyer*."

Naturally James almost spun round at the name but Mike caught him and carried on. "Yes, *THAT* Richard. Always has that table and almost always sits alone most lunch times in the week. He was the boyfriend but by all accounts, he was at least three years older than Jenny; a few locals frowned on their 'close friendship' as it seemed too 'close' to some of a more puritanical nature. Mind you, the parents liked him and pretty much treated him like the son they never had. Word was that he was a gentleman both in public and private and fairly shy around girls of his age.

Now he was still with his mother at the time, and she swore that he was with her the day Jenny disappeared, saying he'd gone down with a bad cold and didn't want to pass it on to Jenny or her family. That was his alibi and frankly we couldn't shake either him nor his mother from that story. But Jenny's disappearance never made sense, especially as they were supposed to meet up." He took a sip from his pint. "I've known many courting couples go to great lengths to still meet up regardless of what they were going through and what their parents thought. Mind you to be honest most disappearances never make any sense and sadly a great many missing persons are never traced or found again.

I've always had this suspicion that he was involved but the biggest problem we had was that we, as in the police and the locals, searched the area from top to bottom and we never found anything suspicious. If you've no body and no evidence to say otherwise, then you have to conclude that she'd run away on the spur of the moment.

There was even a suggestion that perhaps her relationship with her family was not all it was made up to be. Yet, again, there was no proof that they weren't telling us the truth. Especially when her Pa passed on about a year later, most reckon literally of a broken heart, although officially he died of heart failure as I told you the other week. The Portishams were, to all intents and purposes, a very tight and close-knit family and honest to boot as well."

James listened and nodded thoughtfully. "But what if it really was an accident - a simple slip at the wrong moment just as she and Richard were fooling around along the ditch bank. I can see how he would panic thinking he'd be blamed."

He looked down at his shoes thoughtfully then back at Mike. "But why he'd want to cover it up if it was an accident I don't know."

He paused for a moment deep in thought. "Mind you when you consider he would be about eighteen, that would mean they could have been having underage sex, so he'd have been in a lot of trouble with everyone - including her family."

A Ghostly Diversion

Mike nodded. "That was also our thought, but his mother always insisted he was a solid Christian and would never have done anything like that. Even his former schoolteachers and his employer down in Horncastle agreed he was always a shy, polite and considerate young man so we couldn't get that to stick either."

Mike paused, deep in thought himself for a moment. "Tell you what, let's just have a little wander down to the spot you talked about and have a nosey round."

James looked at Mike surprised. "I thought you said we'd be trespassing?"

Mike smiled "I may be retired but my brain cells aren't! I'm sure I can smooth things over if we're caught. Let's go, I assume you'll drive? If so, I'll leave my car here and pick it up later."

They got up and left, apparently not noticing Richard in the corner was deep in discussion with someone on his mobile and had been keeping a wary eye on the two men whilst they had been sat down, deep in their discussion.

#

They arrived at the ditch and James pointed to where Jenny had seemed to use a bridge; indeed, on closer inspection there were signs of wooden struts just about visible, but almost buried under thick grass and a few reeds. Mike explained: "There was a small wooden bridge here that even back then was falling apart. Must have disintegrated at least twenty or thirty years ago now considering how little of it is left. Whatever fell into the ditch seems long gone

A Ghostly Diversion

now". He looked along the overgrown ditch into the distance. "Looks like they're making good progress improving it and getting it back into use. Won't be too long before they reach this section." James had followed his gaze, and, in the distance, a mechanical digger was busy working at enlarging the ditch roughly a mile or so away.

The two men carefully climbed down the bank and managed to avoid the soggy parts at the bottom before climbing up the other side. James pointed towards the tree line.

"About there I reckon - Jenny seemed to be carried into the trees but the first one she seemed to pass straight through." Mike nodded.

"Yes, but look at the trees here at the edge, they're quite young really and I can remember the tree line was a little further back. It's no real surprise it's moved further out towards the ditch. You see the digger in the distance?" Mike pointed along the tree line and the line of the ditch into the distance to his right. James nodded that he could. "The environment agency is having to clear and enlarge this ditch system as they reckon it'll help prevent some of the flooding we've had in recent years. If left unchecked the tree line would steadily move out and eventually encroach on the ditch so I guess the estate must occasionally cut back any more saplings that spring up naturally."

James looked puzzled though.

"Flooding? I know Horncastle has had its unfair share in the past, but I thought that had been sorted - at least that's what our estate agent said!!"

"No, not the town, took a while but that's been sorted. No - just local concerns for the farmland

- it's good land but over the last few years they've ended up losing quite a few crops to becoming waterlogged. They reckon if they bring some of the older, more neglected, ditches back into use they might be able to divert any excess water into a couple of new reservoirs they're building further on. Looks like they're coming along nicely with the work. Won't be long before they're here - then we'd have a long walk round I can tell you as the ditch will be a lot deeper and wider, plus have water in it!"

They moved into the spread of trees and started to fan out looking over the ground as they went. The tree density varied considerably and at times it seemed as though there was a pattern to their distribution.

Half an hour passed, and James had lost sight of Mike but he did notice there seemed to be a pattern to the ground itself - as if there was either channels or possibly the remains of buried walls but they were so low to the ground they could have been natural. He was about to call out for Mike when...

"OI!!" A voice shouted at him.

James jumped in surprise and spun round to see a tall chap with a mousy moustache pushing through the undergrowth towards him.

"This is private ground; what do you think you're doing eh?" The chap glared at James and pulled slightly on his tweed cap.

"Err sorry - I was just exploring, heard there were ruins around here somewhere and I'm into old structures so..."

Tweed cap man butted in. " 'Ere, you're the chap in the mist who thought he saw a ghost aren't you? " He didn't wait for a reply, "I did meet your

A Ghostly Diversion

misses and told her there was to be no trespassin' mind, told her and her mate, bloke who was with you that misty night. No excuse if ya ask me to go trampling around other people's property without care at what damage you might do."

James looked round wondering what damage he had done but couldn't see any and was about to say so when someone else butted in.

"Now, now Charles, he's with me." Mike stepped into view from a dense stand of shrubs off to their right.

"Bloody hell - MIKE FRESHMAN, I ain't seen you for years, detective sir!" Mike smiled and stepped closer offering his hand and the two men shook warmly.

"I'm actually retired now Charles; I see you've met James." Charles looked a bit sheepish, turned to James and nodded. Mike continued "So let me see - what sort of coincidence is it that we're out here in the middle of nowhere and you turn up?"

Charles looked down at his feet, took his cap off and scratched absently at his forehead. Then looked about from side to side.

"Well, like, I still check around the area when I can you see as I've heard there's been folk trampling over the crops willy nilly without any thought of using the proper paths. An' I heard someone had been seen here today so I came over. "

Something told Mike that wasn't quite it though.

"We're not in the fields though Charles, there's no crops, wrong season and we're in the woods - they're not exactly cultivated, are they?" Mike looked squarely into Charles's eyes "Richard

phoned you, didn't he?" Charles was clearly uncomfortable now
and rocked a little to and fro on his heels.

"Well, like I said, I did get to hear there was maybe someone coming over and he thought they might be up to no good, so I had to come, you see, to check for me self."

Mike smiled.

"No problem Charles, we'll be on our way anyhow, so you'll have done your job won't you?"

"Ahh guess I will 'ave done that, aye. So, you'll be away now then?" Mike nodded and motioned to James to follow him, but James hesitated.

"May I ask you if you yourself have seen the ghost of a young woman around these parts?"

Charles looked a little perturbed by the question and scratched his chin.

"Can't say that I have, but I have seen something like a bloke dressed up like you see on some of these ere historical dramas on TV, fancy and the suchlike. But not seen anything for a few years now and reckon I imagined it. But haven't seen a lass at all.

Mind, some years back, a few folks reckoned they'd seen the ghost of the lass that upped an' disappeared back in the early sixties but ah reckon they must have been on summat! Anyhow, I'll be off but will be back later to check you're not snooping around still."

James and Mike both smiled and nodded at Charles as they made their way up out of a hollow past a large tree dangling its roots as if perched precariously on an edge. They headed back towards the road to James' car. Charles watched them go, turned and walked away to the other side of the wood to his dark green Range Rover parked on a dirt track parallel to the wood. Once inside he looked about then made a quick call before driving off.

As Mike and James got into the car Mike chuckled turning to James as he started the car and they drove off down the lane.

"I expected we'd get company soon enough. I noticed Richard was keeping tabs on us back at the inn and spotted him make a quick call. I'd bet he saw we turned towards Grasceby and figured we might be heading to the cottage. Him and Charles go back a long way, old time friends and the like, so I wanted to see if we would get visited at the site.

If there's nothing to hide, then why get someone to turn up when we went snooping around? Bet Marcus overheard a little of what we were saying and tipped him off as well - he's another old family friend of Richard's - nice chap though so I don't think he's actually involved. I doubt Charles is either - he's one of those who really would struggle to keep a secret, especially if it involved a missing girl."

He fell silent as he watched the road wind its way into and through Grasceby.

"OK James, I have to say it's not so much your ghost sightings and story but the odd actions of Richard today that for me is telling its own story. Problem is it's doubtful I could persuade anyone at the station to look into, what is after all, a fifty-year-old missing person case. Leave it with me though and I'll see what I can dig up in the meantime. Drop us off at the inn and I'll be in touch."

James nodded and thanked him as they reached the inn's car park once again. Mike got out of the car and as the retired detective strode over to his own vehicle James noticed the Merc had departed the
inn. James drove towards the entrance and stopped, almost turning back towards the village and on to the cottage but then decided against it and turned for Horncastle and home, his mind mulling over what had happened in the last hour.

15: To the Manor, not born…

The next day as usual Helen had the answer. "Mike may be good, but how about taking a different approach and finding out more about the area near to the cottage. Isn't there supposed to be the remains of a Manor or something large nearby?" James beamed at her over the breakfast table and put his half-eaten toast down on the plate.

"Yeah - I used that as an excuse to that old doddery estate manager but didn't know about a manor, just made it up. It'd be interesting to see where it is supposed to lie and what's left of it now. Where we were looking yesterday was odd and I did wonder if some of the shapes and gullies were buried ruins. I'll check it online tonight to see if anything crops up. Best get off to work, Mark was a bit grumpy yesterday so I'll get in a bit early, might cheer him up to see how eager I am. I'd mention it to Craig but it's his day off today."

He looked at her and realised she was still in her dressing gown "You at work today?" he asked quizzically forgetting her rota and for a fleeting moment she seemed to hesitate.

"No, Charlotte wanted a swap so I'm in tomorrow instead." James smiled at her as he approached the door.

"Oh OK, I'll see you at teatime then love." And he stepped outside to the car. Helen looked out the window, watched him drive off and picked up her phone to make a call.

A Ghostly Diversion

\#

At the office Mark was still a bit grumpy but did acknowledge James arriving well before everyone else, other than himself of course. Lunchtime came and knowing the boss was originally a local man James knocked hesitantly on Mark's office door and heard a gruff 'come in'. He entered thinking he should really not bother Mark with his simple questions. He must have looked apprehensive as Mark smiled, not a common occurrence it had to be said.

"All right - what do you want Jim?" He asked and James started to relax, although slightly annoyed as he hated that nickname.

"Got a moment? It's not related to work but it's lunchtime and I wanted to pick your brain about something."

Mark leaned back in his chair and briefly looked as if he was going to lecture James, then he smiled broadly.

"Course Jim, what's up then? Wife problem, car trouble, inland revenue thinks you're actually rich and want more tax off you?

You've realised you don't work hard enough for me?

All of the above?"

James smiled mockingly and nodded negatively.

"None of that, and I definitely pull my weight around here, just have to put up with a cheeky boss that's all." He cocked his head and looked at Mark expecting a sarcastic retort, but Mark just laughed and agreed James was certainly a worker and he himself was perhaps a bit too cheeky at times.

James launched into his question. "You're originally a local man, you know anything about an old, ruined manor at Grasceby by any chance?"

Mark looked puzzled and James thought maybe Mark had thought something was really wrong or that James was speaking a foreign language.

"Not really, not my thing, history and such things." He looked thoughtfully towards the window and carried on. "Can't remember anything being mentioned in school either but then I didn't take much notice in history class, not with Stella to take my mind off school. Glad she wasn't into mathematics or science otherwise I'd never have learnt anything…"

James must have had a blank face on him as Mark quickly added "Now the wife of course." He winked at James in a wicked sort of way. "I expect you've drawn a blank with the web then?"

James shrugged.

"I've only really thought about it this morning, didn't have time before coming to work; just thought I'd ask if you knew anything first." Mark swivelled slightly in his chair and motioned for James to come round to his side of the desk.

"I'm bored at the moment so as you've still got ten minutes of break left let's take a look-see then." He pulled his head mike into position. "Search mode, query string, *'Grasceby Manor'*." He commanded and the screen showed his quite fancy system begin the search and immediately stop with a result. James whistled in approval, he knew the boss always had the best equipment, Mark waved to indicate there was probably more info and put his hand over the microphone.

"This says the manor is currently occupied, so that can't be right. Oh, I see, there's a manor situated *in* the village. It's around two hundred years old so it's seen a bit of history then but probably not the one you want."

"Yeah, I knew about the 'modern' manor in the village, but does it mention anything before it?"

"Give me a mo, search mode, query string, '*old Grasceby Manor*', query string '*Grasceby Manor ruins*'." He commanded again and the system spun into action again only taking moments this time to display around a hundred thousand results! "Ooo looks like fun and games..." He muttered under his breath as he scrolled manually down the list, but James eyes were ahead of him and pointed to a link.

"Try that one about 'the original De Grasceby Manor." Mark followed the link but noticed James was leaning over a little too closely for his liking. He leaned back a little forcing James to move and then Mark touched a button on his desk and the large wall screen came to life.

"I wondered if you'd use that." Remarked James and he smiled at Mark, but it was clear his boss was skim reading the text and images, deep in concentration.

"Remember you've got just six more minutes of my and your spare time left so let's get to the bottom of this." He picked up his mini tablet and tapped to enlarge the text on screen and they both walked over to the wall and read the passage.

A Ghostly Diversion

'Grasceby Manor, or to give it its proper title, the 'De Grasceby Manor', is not to be confused with the later 'Grasceby Manor' situated within the small village of Grasceby in central Lincolnshire. The original manor was built by Charles De Grasceby, a wealthy French aristocrat. De Grasceby relocated from Paris with his family to the farming county of Lincolnshire in England in 1716 despite the normal hatred between the two countries. Some authorities of that period argue it is not fully understood why such a move took place but if later events were anything to go by De Grasceby was probably hounded out of his parent country and so sought refuge in England.

It should also be noted that another theory adds that De Grasceby was publicly vocal against the French attempt at crowning the Old Pretender, James Stuart, as King of England in 1715. This move would certainly see him becoming unpopular in his own country and may explain why he was allowed to come over to Lincolnshire by the eventually crowned King George I. The King awarded him with an estate and an allowance for his support.

De Grasceby had salvaged a good proportion of his wealth by smuggling many valuables out of France across the channel and he went on to commission the building of a grand Manor for his family between Horncastle, Wragby and Bardney along with a few dwellings nearby for his servants. The latter became the original site for Grasceby village.

It is believed the Manor was only partially completed however, as it soon became clear that Charles was a wanton gambler and lost most of the estate lands he'd been given by the King along with a large part of his fortune. The family struggled whilst living in the unfinished manor and gradually their servants abandoned them to seek better employment elsewhere.

A Ghostly Diversion

When George II succeeded his father to the throne in 1727 the new King had no love for De Grasceby, detesting the Frenchman. Eventually De Grasceby fled England but there are no records of where he and his family went. Popular belief was that they drowned when several ships capsized in the English Channel around the same period of time but there has never been any proof offered to support this theory.

Meanwhile, left unattended and unwanted, the manor fell into disrepair and was never used again. The nearby village also deteriorated but a few loyal villagers moved approximately a mile (confirmation required here as there is little documentary evidence to support this reference to distance) to a better location, founding the current village of Grasceby using stonework scavenged from both the original village and the manor.

Few surviving documents or maps show the exact location of the original manor although it is hoped that future advances in technology may at least help in locating and confirming its site.

The modern Grasceby Manor was founded around ten years after the foundation of the new village and like the village is not near the presumed original site. The current owners of the man...'

Mark looked at his world clock and raised an eyebrow at the time it showed.

"Not much else there my friend and looks like we got a bit carried away as it's over five minutes after lunchtime!"

James though looked well pleased with what they'd found.

"Can I have a hard copy of that Mark?" His boss nodded.

"It was more interesting than I thought it'd be - perhaps I should have taken more notice of Miss Harley when she droned on about history at school". He smiled, downloaded the data to James's workstation and with a small wave as a hint, James went back to work.

#

Helen stepped out of her car and looked around nervously. She still wasn't sure why she was doing this but something deep inside of her compelled her to continue. She knocked on the door and almost changed her mind and walked away, but then Craig opened the door.

"I wasn't sure if you were going to come" he said and smiled at her nervously. Beckoning to her she followed him into the house, and he took her coat, noticing the delicate blouse and skirt she was wearing. Once again that perfume he'd noticed just a few weeks back wafted into his nostrils.

"You sure you want to do this now?" She asked and Craig smiled and nodded, indicating towards the sofa or chair, her choice. She thanked him and sat down on the soft chair and crossed her legs pulling the skirt down over her knees. "I've done some research already and it seems you were right and wrong at the same time."

"What do you mean?" He asked and Helen fished out a series of folders from her bag and placed them on the coffee table.

"Although you are right about your surname being French sounding it's actually a corruption of an older Prussian surname so I guess you could say you may have Germanic origins." She opened one of the folders and leafed through several papers and handed them to him.

Craig leaned forward and started looking through them as Helen began to relax a little and settle back into her chair. "It's quite fascinating really. I've been into family history for a few years now and you can get quite carried away with the research. I'm now back to about the seventeenth century if I was strict with the family records for my family tree but if you don't mind having a few assumptions and a little leeway you could claim to go back much further. I've got your tree back to 1824 so far and I'm sure there's more we can still do."

"Oh wow, Helen, that's amazing. I really am thrilled with this. You must tell me what I owe you, you can't do this for free you know."

He looked at her again reclining in the chair and a guilty feeling swept over him as her skirt seemed to have slipped up a little and he looked away towards the door to his kitchen. "Err, would you like a coffee or perhaps tea?"

Helen nodded and indicted tea for her and as Craig got up to leave, she shuffled in her seat and made herself more comfortable. She heard him scurrying around in the kitchen and the kettle duly boiled. Drinks made, Craig brought them through on his favourite tray, one showing medieval castles on, he hoped Helen would be impressed with his choice. He noticed she'd changed seat and was now on the sofa so he put the tray down and began towards the chair, but Helen spoke up.

"I don't bite you know, at least not according to James."

A Ghostly Diversion

She, and indeed Craig, hesitated at the mention of James but he shrugged and sat next to her as she fetched out a few more documents. Helen shuffled closer to Craig and motioned at a particular A4 sized paper she had put on the coffee table in front of him. He peered at it with interest but couldn't help but be distracted by Helen's perfume.

She nudged him back to reality and held the paper in her hand, but Craig didn't hear her words as he realised that he was not really paying attention to the paper. From out the corner of his eye her chest kept heaving, betraying the outline of her bra as she talked enthusiastically about a distant possible relation he had. He really couldn't concentrate then suddenly realised she was no longer talking to him.

Their eyes met.

Thoughts and emotions collided full on and suddenly they were kissing passionately.

#

Helen returned home later that afternoon. She knew that something profound had happened, a shift, an emotional realisation, and an overwhelming sense that her world was changing. What's more, she was prepared to let it change, for good or for bad.

Somehow, she managed to give no sign to James that anything was amiss when he arrived back from work that evening all excited, but in her heart she wondered if anything would ever be the same again.

After their meal James showed Helen what he and Mark had found about De Grasceby and his Manor.

A Ghostly Diversion

"All well and good." she said. "But you still need to find out exactly where the old manor was located and if there really is a link between where this 'Jenny' lies and any ruins. It seems plain to me that you have to see if there are any old maps that go back far enough to show it, but personally I'm doubtful."

James listened and sat thoughtful for a few moments.

"Yes - it could be a wild goose chase really. I'll go upstairs and log on to see if I can find any historical mapping apps."

Helen nodded and he got up and left the room whilst she got out her smart phone and began messaging Craig about meeting up. She saw the reply and texted back, 'luv u 2 xx' but couldn't help looking towards the stairs as a wave of guilt swept over her.

Upstairs it didn't take James long to find several online sites for old maps - but the tiny example maps were useless. What's more, to get higher resolution maps online, he had to register and pay to use the services. He sighed but thought 'why not' and filled in the appropriate details on the most promising site. Ten minutes later he had a vast archive to explore but it took another half hour to sift through a variety of epochs, coordinates, and map scales.

Pouring backwards through several 'layers' of historical maps he began to realise that the level of detail he needed was simply not available. Nothing showed up in a radius of five or ten miles out from the modern location of Grasceby or close to 'Wolds View'. He leaned back in his chair allowing the multi layered map in front of him to blur for a moment as he rested his eyes.

Lines.

Regular lines and rectangles.

A few triangles. Basically, field boundaries.

Patterns.

Unusual patterns, he noted. He looked again at the screen and started to notice a few strangely shaped boundaries. At the side of the map there were a couple of options he'd not yet added, mainly because he wasn't sure what they'd tell him but now he clicked on one for visual satellite data.

Something stood out perhaps around half a mile north northeast of the location of 'Wolds View' Cottage. A clumpiness in the landscape, an unusual collection of almost rectangular shapes merging into a small wood. The wood he and Mike had explored the other day he quickly realised...

Enlarging the view didn't help much, until he removed the clutter of the mapping layers just to leave the satellite. He muttered to himself as he added an infrared view but the view was spoiled and he realised it was dominated by vegetation and a good proportion of what could be the site was in the wood and obscured. Scanning round the page he clicked the button marked Lidar only for a pop-up box appearing to inform him that the option was only available to Platinum users. Huh, more expense he thought to himself.

Lidar was a relatively new tool to archaeologists, instrumental in discovering tens of thousands of previously undiscovered archaeological sites across the world and he was sorely tempted. Clicking again he sat back when he noticed the price but after only a brief hesitation, he entered the details needed and the Lidar button became active.

He clicked to bring in the overlay and took a sharp intake of breath so loud that Helen came rushing upstairs to find out if everything was OK.

"Will you take a look at *this.*" He said and pointed to the screen.

"Wow - now that is impressive, so what am I looking at?" She quipped but before he could say anything derogatory, she laughed. "That has to be the old Manor then?"

The Lidar map showed a collection of what could only be foundations of a large building with various out buildings around it. Using the cursor James slid the map to the left and down a little and a second much smaller set of foundations came into view to the upper right "And the old village." She added in a whisper.

James moved the view back to the original mass of foundations. Noting the overlay with the visible satellite image he could see that the ruined buildings didn't extend to the edge of the present-day outline of the wood, consistent with what Mike had suspected. However, something else piqued his interest.

There was a long and narrow channel or very thin structure extending southwards from what appeared to be the largest south facing room. Zooming in further didn't help as it was at the limit of the Lidar resolution but zooming a little out, he and Helen could see that whatever it was extended almost to a gnat's whisker of the ditch close to where James had seen Jenny being carried into the wood.

A Ghostly Diversion

"Wonder why Mike and I didn't see that; we must have been right over it and in fact must have followed some of it without knowing it for a short distance before we spread out."

"Centuries of undergrowth building up to cover it I guess." Helen offered. She then noticed the printer had printed a slip that looked like a receipt, and she picked it up and gasped again. "You paid all that? Tell you what, it comes out of your pocket not mine or the house account for that matter!" She scowled at him and lightly clipped him about his right ear.

"Yeah, yeah, I know - worth it though if you ask me - it allows me to save the maps to the system so at least I can keep what I've found."

Helen looked at him and shrugged.

"Well, I'm off to bed - coming?" She saw the look on his face and quickly added "To sleep!"

James smiled wryly and nodded. It was getting late after all and tomorrow was Saturday so no work for a couple of days, bliss!

#

Several miles away though and completely unaware of what James had discovered, Jenny wandered once again along her old route. Every so often for some reason she felt compelled to retrace her final sad moments. After her poor attempt to project herself had ended up making James collapse at his place of work she'd been reluctant to try to seek him out that way and wished he would come back to the cottage.

A Ghostly Diversion

She'd not seen James or felt his presence in the cottage for a couple of weeks now and she sighed as she wondered if she'd ever be free of the old world and whether he would come back and help her move onto the next life…

16: To dig or not to dig…

The next few weeks began to drag as James received no word from Mike, despite sending him everything he had found about the location of the old Manor. However, the Lincolnshire Archaeological Society were more interested and invited James to give a presentation at a meeting later in the year. They were also looking at applying for funds for exploratory excavations to take place and had been in contact with the Grasceby estate with positive signs from them. It seemed that the positive publicity the estate would get would help offset an area of good land being dug up for several months.

Unfortunately, the weather had other ideas.

The autumn rains really hammered the whole country let alone their adopted county. Despite Lincolnshire being regarded as one of the driest counties of the UK, being as it was on the eastern side of England, it didn't escape the downpours or localised flooding. It hampered the expansion of the drainage ditch near Grasceby which was, ironically of all things, continually beset by waterlogging. It slowed the work down, much to the chagrin of the locals, the environment agency and the workmen involved.

Before James and Helen knew it, Christmas was suddenly upon everyone and as they'd become firm friends, Craig came over and spent a lot of it with them, much to Helen's delight, it seemed to James. Especially at the firm's Christmas party held at the Star and Crescent Moon Inn, a suggestion James had put forward, but with Helen dancing a lot

A Ghostly Diversion

with Craig that evening, he had started to regret it. He didn't want to think the unthinkable though and pushed thoughts of Helen being unfaithful to the back of his mind.

New Year rolled by and of course once it was over the snow came down causing more travel chaos, although the kids in the local villages were delighted at the time off from school. Several times when the snow was at its deepest and roads were blocked by drifts Helen had received texts saying her social meetings were cancelled and her reactions seemed a little over the top when she dropped into black moods after a few of the messages.

A couple of times James visited 'Wolds View' but on his second visit the green Range Rover was there, and he'd had another run in with Charles, so he'd decided not to visit until the weather improved. Especially as the snow meant his footsteps could be seen wandering all around the grounds and round to the back door!

February remained icy with occasional wintry blasts of snow. March beckoned beset with more of the same, then slipped into April. For a couple of short weeks everyone enjoyed a dash of early spring warm sunshine and James' thoughts again turned to calling round to 'Wolds View' to see if Jenny was still waiting for him.

Helen was no longer interested in, as she called it, 'James' obsession' with a ghostly girl so she spent more and more time out in the evenings at her various 'social' events.

Or at least that's what she told James.

He knew she now frequented several social media sites, something she always used to say was a waste of people's time. James happened to agree with her on this which is why her interest in them seemed at odds with her past behaviour. He tried not to be suspicious but knew something was wrong. He remembered how she'd been when she thought he had been having an affair so he just couldn't bring himself to spy on her. He was probably imagining it he told himself but deep inside he knew, and his heart was heavy.

One lunchtime though the past and present were suddenly thrown together in a messy tangle. James phone buzzed at work, and he picked it up to hear an excited Helen struggling to get her words out.

"Helen, Helen, HELEN! Slow down love, what is it?"

"Turn on the local news - they've found her!!" She almost shouted over the connection.

"What do you mean, found he.. Bloody hell - is she alive then?" he asked, confused, as he knocked on Mark's office door and heard him say "enter". He did so and quickly asked Mark to turn his main wall screen onto the local newsfeed channel. It burst into life mid story. A heavy-set man with a safety hat on was talking live to a female reporter. Incredibly they looked to be close to where James and Mike had explored near the woods what seems like ages in the past, back in October.

".. were making good progress in the current dry weather when one of the diggers uncovered a tunnel as it excavated the north side of the ditch. We weren't really that bothered by it at first as we sometime come across old forgotten walls and such like but when the boss, Mr Coates, took a closer look he found the bones and old clothing. That's when we called in the police and now of course we can't get on with the job as they've cordoned it off."

The camera swung round to the reporter.

"And did you suspect foul play when you realised that they were human remains?"

Cameraman swung back to the workman.

"No, not really - could be any explanation I guess - I'll leave that to the experts, I just want to get on with me job." The camera cut to the reporter again and she turned to speak into it.

"So, there you have it Patrick, rumours abound already that it could be the remains of a young girl who went missing over fifty years ago but we have no confirmation yet that the remains are even female. I'm Emma Frasier, back to you in the studio, Patrick."

The presenter in the studio turned away from his screen to face the camera.

"Well, we've managed to get hold of Chief Inspector Wills of Lincolnshire Police for his views." Patrick turned back to his screen and continued. "Chief Inspector thank you for joining us at short notice. Tell me, are you in any position this early on to tell us more about these human remains and who they may belong to?" The camera switched to the Inspector who was trying to clear his throat.

"Hello Patrick, I can confirm very little at this early stage. I have a brief statement to give though if I may, based on what we do know so far." He paused briefly and got his breath as he looked at his sheet.

"This morning at nine twenty-three am, a freelance company working for the environment agency, working to enlarge and improve the drainage near to the village of Grasceby, Lincolnshire, accidentally uncovered, what at this stage, appears to be some form of tunnel that appears to head northwards into the nearby wood.

On closer inspection the team leader, Mr Phillip Coates, noticed a human skull, several other bones and the remains of clothing inside. He followed correct procedures by stopping all work and notifying his superiors and indeed the local constabulary." He paused and lowered the piece of paper he'd been reading from.

"We have closed off the area and as shown in your report, we now have a protective enclosure in place so that our forensic team can make a thorough examination of the scene. I hope to be able to bring you further information later today from Detective Superintendent Sally Fieldman who is in charge of the investigation.

I must stress that at this stage we cannot say whether there is any connection with the case that your reporter referred to in that earlier report." He was about to say something else, but the screen suddenly went blank and James looked round thinking a problem had occurred. Mark was looking at him quizzically though.

"Care to explain what that has to do with our work?" He asked and James squirmed and searched for what to say.

"Err - remember when some months back before Christmas we were looking into where the old Grasceby Manor was located?" Mark thought for a second or two then smiled and nodded.

"Err, yes, I remember that, what of it?" he asked.

"Well, I did more research, didn't you see the report about the Archaeological society on the local news just after Christmas that mentioned me?" Mark though looked blank.

"No, remember - I'm not really into history - duh!"

James winced but launched into what he'd discovered about the manor and then tentatively sketched out a very brief version of his ghostly encounters with Jenny and the investigation he'd done with Mike Freshman.

"You have got to be pulling my pisser!" Mark exclaimed and got up, walked round the table and put a gentle hand on James' shoulder. "You know me, I'm quite, how shall we say, tolerant of silly stories like that. But for over eight or more months now there's been something about you that's different, something on your mind but more purposeful, determined, call it what you like, but apparently not concerning work..."

He was about to continue when James' phone buzzed and a quick glance down at the display told both of them it was someone James wanted to talk to right now.

Mark looked at him questioningly, "You going to just ignore that?" Said Mark and James shook his head but before he spoke Mark interrupted, "I've known you for some years now Jim and you wouldn't do this as a prank. I can see it's that Mike detective chap you've just mentioned. Take the afternoon off - I can cover for you. But let me know what happens - you never know how we might be able to use the possible publicity if one of our own can help the investigation."

James didn't need telling twice; quickly thanking Mark, he hurried off to get his coat.

17: Face to face…

They met up at 'Wolds View' Cottage which seemed particularly eerie this time. Mike hurried over to James and shook his hand.

"Well, this is a turn up for the books, by the sounds of it you were right as to where Jenny lay all these years."

"So, they've definitely identified her then?" James asked, but Mike shook his head.

"No, but there's too much coincidence for me. I've heard via my own, let's say old channels, they've already confirmed it is a female and that she's between 15 and 18 years old so close enough to Jenny's age of 16. They haven't informed the local investigating officer yet.

Also, the location, come on, it's too close to the cottage and about right if someone did kill her nearby as you suggest. Come with me, if fortune is on our side, we might be able to get a look at the crime scene considering this used to be my patch."

They walked, ironically as James noted, along the same route he'd watched, and followed, Jenny take and… was that a chill in the air almost as if someone was following behind them? He hesitantly glanced back…

…to see Jenny following them and he couldn't help but smile. She smiled back at him then faded from view as he almost stumbled, not looking where he was putting his feet.

"Watch your step James, it's a bit messy here now that the experts have descended, they're already churning up the field with their vans and equipment."

Mike hadn't noticed James looking back and smiling.

"I tell you what though, I'll eat my hat if they are able to say if she did break her neck just as you said she had." James just murmured agreement as they reached the police cordon and the officer on duty warily watched them approach. He came forward to stop them, holding his hand up to them. A young constable, probably only been out of training a year or two so he was keen to do his job.

"Sorry gents but we can't have sightseers or reporters on site. Any questions you may have will have to go through the proper channels."

Mike looked at him and smiled.

"Ahh yes, good to see you doing your job officer. I'm Detective Inspector Michael Freshman - *retired*." He fished out his old ID and showed it to the officer. "Can you just fetch who's in charge for a quick word? This used to be my case." The young policeman looked at him then using his police com link made a quick call mentioning Mike's name and rank. He nodded as he listened to the person on the other end then turned back to Mike.

"If you'll just wait here sir, she'll be along in a moment."

Mike smiled as if knowing who it was going to be and turned to say something to James when he stopped and looked past him, and his face took on a serious aspect.

James's heart leapt into his mouth thinking Mike had at last seen Jenny.

"James, turn slowly round." James began to turn as instructed anticipating Mike admitting he could see the ghost for himself. "Tell me if you recognise the car through the hedge a bit back from where we've parked."

James hid his disappointment but did as he was told. Just about visible he could just make out a dark metallic blue ...

James turned back to Mike.

"He's here and if I'm right I bet he's bricking it!"

Mike nodded but they were then interrupted as a plain clothed, but very attractive, red-haired woman, in perhaps her mid to late thirties, approached and called out. James vaguely recalled seeing her at Horncastle police station some months back, before Christmas when he'd first gone in to ask about Mike Freshman.

"They dragged you out of retirement for this then Mike?" The red head called out.

Mike began to turn round but didn't need to see the person to know who she was.

"Now Sally, is that the way to talk to your former boss and mentor?" He motioned to James and indicated to each of them in turn. "James Hansone meet Superintendent Sally Petersan."

Sally coughed for attention.

"Excuse me Mike, *wrong* on two counts, '*Detective*' Superintendent if you will, plus I'm divorced so it's back now officially to Sally Fieldman if you please."

Mike smiled at the latter and raised his eyebrows.

"Oh, does that mean I'm now in with a chance?"

A Ghostly Diversion

"Yeah, humour wasn't your best strength was it." She retorted whilst James listened and watched the friendly banter take place between them.

"So, my teaching paid off, made detective after all then. Force must be getting worse since I left."

Sally looked at him scornfully.

"Cheeky bugger!" She retorted but then leant in, hugged Mike and whispered something in his ear. Mike smiled again and chuckled a little. Sally looked at James then back to Mike.

"So, let me guess, it's about the Portisham case, isn't it? Hoped you'd pop up when they announced the discovery of a body so close to her old home. The case never left you, did it? We haven't actually confirmed it is her though at this stage." She turned to look James over, "However can I just clarify why you're here Mr Handsome before we proceed?"

Before James could say a word though to correct her Mike butted in.

"He's with me, a consultant if you will, and between us we'd almost got to the point of asking you pros to take a new and fresh look at the evidence again." He leaned closer and it was his turn to speak into her ear, "Go along with me on this one Sally, you know what my instincts were like."

Sally looked thoughtfully at James then nodded.

"OK for the moment, but if my boss decides to visit then he's out of here - got that Mr Handsome?" She looked at James and smiled disarmingly. He realised her mistake again.

"It's err, Hansone, not Handsome actually and thank you, I..."

She cut him off mid stumble.

"A slight difference but not far off the mark really."

With that Sally looked over at Mike and winked mischievously. Turning, she indicated for them to follow as she nodded to the constable to let them through, and he lifted the cordon tape up for them to pass under. They walked up to the protective enclosure surrounding the location of the body. It was a bit lopsided having to also partially cover the ditch making it look somewhat ungainly and certainly out of place.

She lifted up the enclosure entrance flap and they went in. On a makeshift table on the ground to the right side of the broken roof of the tunnel, the almost completely decomposed body was laid out. A woman dressed in white coveralls and wearing a face mask was bent over taking a close look at the remains and looked up at them. She nodded at Sally putting her right thumb up then carried on with her examination.

"It's OK Harriet, they're with me but we'll not get in your way." Sally said and they heard a muffled 'OK' from the other person. Sally turned and whispered to the two men.

"That's Harriet, our forensics expert, don't cross her when she's busy."

"Didn't have that sort of thing in my day." Mike nodded and smiled as he whispered back.

What remained of some skin and dark hair still clung to sections of the skull and a few other bones further down the body. Remains of clothing

A Ghostly Diversion

also clung to large parts and the low-cut blue top and summery style flower covered skirt were plain to see, if soiled and wet. At the side was a pile of other clothes covered in places with dirt and what appeared to be either algae or mould.

James went cold and thought he was going to be sick. Both Mike and Sally noticed him as he wavered a little and stopped short of reaching the table.

"You okay James?" Mike asked as he touched and gently held James' elbow to stop him swaying. Sally looked at James with a puzzled expression on her face.

"It's…it's…all suddenly real. Up to now it's felt like just a story, and I was going to wake up and everything would be fine but..." He trailed off and turned and walked back outside shaking his head. Mike and Sally followed him out and Sally was frowning. Harriet was just pleased the distractions had left her in peace to get on with her work.

Sally wasn't amused.

"Can you guys fill me in please, this is the first time anyone not connected to the crime scene has seen the body and I'd like to know what you mean by that comment?"

Mike looked at James. "You okay now?" He asked. James nodded and took a few deep breaths and stared back towards where he could just see parts of the cottage through the trees. He found some resolve deep down and turned back to them, took a deep breath and went back inside with the other two following him.

"Yes, sorry about that." He walked slowly around the body much to Harriet's annoyance. "It's

A Ghostly Diversion

her alright, the clothes are identical, but I don't see the hair clip, I guess it must be somewhere in the tunnel." Mike nodded his head knowingly then turned to Sally before she could say anything.

"You really need to bear with me on this Sally as there are two things to what James has told me that was *never* in the public domain. It's with regards to the details we released to the public when we asked people to be on the lookout for a certain missing girl."

"I assume you do mean the Jennifer Portisham case back in your early days?" Suggested Sally and Mike nodded again.

"Yes, it's always bugged me we never found her, and I didn't buy the idea she'd run away. You see there was a small, almost invisible, black hair clip which got missed off the details we put out in the missing person's brief. Sloppy, I know, but you'd barely notice it unless you were right next to her. We concentrated on the most easily identifiable features, hair colour and general style, the dimple on her right cheek and of course her clothes that she was last seen in before vanishing.

But we *NEVER* made the hair clip public, and I can't remember anyone else ever mentioning it. Plus, these are not the clothes her mother said she was wearing the last time she saw her. Yet only two people have ever mentioned the exact description of the clothes this body is wearing, Marcus Crabbe and James here.

Until this man came to me a few months back. He gave a description that included a brief mention of the hair clip and the clothes, and I can tell you, I don't buy it that Marcus is involved. He's a blabber mouth at the best of times and could never have kept this a secret."

He turned to James. "Sorry about the long delay over winter when I didn't get back to you, but I went over and over my old case notes, checked through the police archives and there was no mention of the hair clip in them or in the notes and newspaper cuttings I'd kept about it. I remembered it from the original interrogation of Jenny's father and mother by my predecessor, but it didn't seem relevant at the time. So, when you mentioned it, I made a few enquiries to see if you were alive back then."

James looked at him stunned but Mike carried on. "I know - you weren't even born then, and you don't really look old enough, but I needed to completely rule you out because there was only four other people who knew her well enough to know about the hair clip, her mother and father, her boyfriend and his mother."

Sally looked puzzled though.

"What hair clip? There's nothing like that either on the body or in the tunnel where she was found. Anyway, we haven't had confirmation it is 'your' Jenny." Mike patted her on the shoulder.

"Bear with me. My contacts have confirmed it's her."

Sally looked distinctly annoyed at this and pursed her lips as if to admonish him, but he continued quickly on before she had the chance. "When I was just a mere sapling of a constable, Detective Inspector Gerald Heath conducted the investigation, and I was with him taking notes when he interviewed Jenny's parents. 'Old GH' as we called him did most of the interviews, but I was with him on all of them.

They told us that the previous Christmas the family had pulled crackers, as you do, and in Jenny's was a cheap and cheerful hair clip. Her boyfriend Richard had bought the crackers as part of his contribution to the celebrations as he'd been invited to Christmas dinner that year along with his mother. The hair clip was in the cracker that he and Jenny pulled so it was special to her. From then on Jenny always wore it - even though to us it would be quite tacky, but remember she was, at that stage just under sixteen and she didn't care."

James butted in.

"I can remember seeing she had the hair clip." James turned to Sally. "But you say, detective, that there isn't one now - so where is it?"

Sally was getting somewhat frustrated.

"Just *what* is your connection with all this and how did you know about the hair clip then?" She fumed. Mike put his hand on her arm.

"I mean it - trust me for now. He's right though, where is the clip? Now I can immediately think of at least two possibilities. One: it fell out when she fell down the ditch and her neck was broken an.."

Sally looked as if she was going to explode.

"WHOA THERE! How do you know she's got a broken neck - Harriet's only told me just before you two turned up! Let me guess" she looked accusingly at James "- bloody contacts!" Mike smiled at her in a disarming way.

"I'll come to that. And no, they didn't tell me. As I was saying, secondly: the person who was with her, and most probably killed her, has the clip or at least took it at the time."

James looked in deep thought whilst Sally was clearly becoming annoyed that she wasn't getting the full story about James. James looked at each of them in turn, ending with Mike.

"There was a glint from her hair as she was being carried into the woods - she must have had the hair clip still in place when she was placed in the tunnel." Sally passed her limit and put her hands firmly on her shapely hips.

"That's it, OUTSIDE both of you NOW!" Sally ordered them and pointed in the direction of the entrance flap as Harriet watched on quite bemused at what she was overhearing. The three of them passed under the flap as Sally again appeared on the edge of exploding. Harriet chuckled to herself, turned away and busied herself with the body. The constable at the cordon edge turned to look away knowing you shouldn't mess with Detective Fieldman!

In the distance they heard a car start up and saw a dark metallic blue Mercedes drive off down the lane in the direction of Grasceby. Mike looked at her urgently.

"Put out a call to bring Richard Dreyer in for questioning, Sally." He pulled a dog-eared notepad out his right jacket pocket and quickly leafing through it found the page and showed it to Sally before she could argue. "I'll guarantee that was him in his dark blue Mercedes." Sally though was having none of it.

"*I've* been very patient and I have an investigation to perform as you very well know Det

A Ghostly Diversion

Freshman 'RETIRED' so nothing gets done until *YOU* explain what *HE*" pointing at James, "has to do with all this, wha.."

She was interrupted by a young female assistant who had been sent out by Harriet and handed her a sheaf of papers. She looked down and leafed through them quickly. Her changing expression spoke volumes though to Mike. She looked at him and let out a deep breath. "I always hated it when you were two steps ahead of me in a case." She drew a deep breath in then exhaled quickly in annoyance.

"OK, this confirms it is indeed Jennifer *AND* she probably died due to her neck having been broken. Her clothes match the description her parents gave when they last saw her, oh hang on, they don't!"

Sally scanned down through more notes then nodded thoughtfully. "We've found a second set of clothes in a bundle with the body that do match what her mother last saw her wearing. She must have changed after her parents saw her when they left." She looked squarely at James. "*So*, start talking mister about how you know so much about Jenny and make it snappy as I'm at my limit!"

Mike began to speak but James butted in.

"Sorry Mike but this has to come from me." He went on to explain as succinctly as he could what had happened over the last year. At the end Sally looked blue in the face and was about to protest but Mike cut in.

"*Look*, I didn't believe him at first but there are simply too many things he described that cannot be coincidence or just lucky guesses. He even mentioned the hair clip and pointed roughly to where she was lying buried, although neither of us can see how she could be so close to the ditch. Especially when James claims he saw her being carried into the woods." Sally blew her cheeks out and stood contemplating her next move.

James though became excited.

"Have any of your officers traced the tunnel back into the woods? Perhaps the actual entrance is not at the ditch but part of the original old De Grasceby Manor in the information I sent to you a few weeks back, Mike." He got even more agitated as something shot into his memory from his original research. "In fact, on the Lidar maps I downloaded there is a linear feature running southwards from the old manor down to the ditch that I'd wager matches the tunnel!"

Sally looked at each of them in turn and shook her head.

"I'm going to regret this, I can feel it in my bowels, but come on, follow me. I have an officer looking for the entrance as we speak." With that they walked round and past the covered scene and James began to track back where he thought he remembered the tunnel should be. Just thirty metres in and they found the ground suddenly sloped off right next to a clump of old tree stumps; an officer was bent down with half his body missing under the stumps.

"What is it Dave?" Sally called out to him, and the officer quickly backed out and brushed loose soil and dead leaves off his uniform.

"Sorry Ma'am, you were right. The tree roots must have concealed it well but there is a tunnel and

A Ghostly Diversion

it's the same one. What's more it also looks as if someone fashioned a crude form of doorway that added to its natural look keeping it hidden."

James looked round and began to notice the slight undulations, subtle rises and general shapes the ground made. He looked over to Mike and motioned pointing out the shapes in the terrain.

"This is close to where you and I were a while back when we came looking. We're in the old Manor." He traced several features with his forefinger. "These look like the outlines of long gone and eroded foundations. Wonder why the local archaeologists didn't find this bit when I sent them the maps and details?" Sally looked up from examining the tunnel entrance.

"Too difficult here due to the wood so they started in the field the other side where they could excavate easier. Plus, the estate managers were happier with them digging there rather than disturbing the woods and the wildlife. The field was being left fallow this year, so it didn't matter to them if it was disturbed. Mind you they have a lot on their plate now with a murder scene and the planned ditch scheme is now on hold until we're finished with our investigations."

She reached for her com link as it buzzed, and she walked a few paces away from them talking into it as she went. A few moments later she came back with a wry smile on her face.

"You'll be pleased to know that Richard Dreyer has handed himself in at Horncastle Police station. You'd both best come with me. I WILL get to the bottom of how you are involved in all this Mr Hansone, you can count on it!"

A Ghostly Diversion

Mike looked at James but just smiled as they headed back through the wood towards the crime scene.

18: It was an accident, honest...

Normally it was a pretty quiet police station used to petty burglary and occasional late-night fighting after hours on New Year's Eve, but now it seemed to buzz with activity. Sally, Mike, and James entered but Sally pulled James to the side and motioned to the officer on the desk as she spoke quietly into his left ear.

"I want you to write me a full report with as much detail you can remember starting from the beginning and in particular detailing what you *think* you saw took place."

James began protesting that he didn't *'think'* he saw anything, he *knew*, but she stopped him dead.

"Listen, I could have you arrested for impeding an investigation and potentially wasting police time as there's no scientific proof of, and I don't believe in, ghosts. But you *have* got me intrigued and I've known Mike a helluva long time and I trust him. So be good, humour me and go into that office with Constable Fletcher. Give him your *honest* account of things and he'll take it all down. Mike and I will question Mr Dreyer."

James nodded and after Sally had a brief conversation with the constable, James followed him into a side room. Constable Fletcher though seemed somewhat bemused at the thought of hearing a ghost story as evidence.

#

A Ghostly Diversion

"We've gone through the preliminaries, and you understand about your rights. So, for the record, can you confirm your name is Mr Richard Andrew Dreyer, aged sixty nine living at…" she stopped and raised her eyebrows and looked squarely at him "*'Wolds Cottage'*, Ancaster Road, Horncastle and that you came to this police station of your own free will?"

The person opposite Sally and Mike nodded, then verbally agreed.

"Yes, that's me, Mike can also vouch for that fact."

Sally ignored the last bit and leaned forward towards Dreyer.

"Good. Tell me Mr Dreyer, what is your connection with our investigation concerning what we now know to be the body of a former girlfriend of yours. A Miss Jennifer Portisham, from fifty years ago who vanished and has not been seen until today?"

Richard Dreyer looked pained and for a few moments looked around the room as if trying to think of a way to start.

"You understand, I came in of my own free will. I always wanted to explain everything, but it never felt the right time until now …"

"You mean until you couldn't hide any longer once her body was discovered." Sally interjected.

Dreyer looked sharply at her.

"I never intended… you know, when they found her body." He rambled, then found an inner strength welling up inside. "It… it was a stupid accident. Bloody ditch, if we hadn't been messing about …we could have got married, had a life together, had kids …" His voice trailed off and he looked down at the edge of the table. Mike moved to say something, but Sally reached over and held Dreyer's hands warmly, she'd learned how to get people to talk, her way.

"It's ok, take your time. Go back to the beginning. How did you and Jennifer meet?" Richard looked up and tried to smile as the memories came flooding back.

"School and then again when the circus came to town. We were only kids though; I would be fourteen and she must have been about eleven and like all kids in them days we played games in the playground. I got a bit of a ribbing from me mates as she kept smiling at me and I just loved the attention from her. Something about her eyes, they were so…deep, mesmerising, loving."

Dreyer's attention seemed to drift away lost as his thoughts turned back to those eyes of Jenny's.

Sally gently squeezed his hand and he looked up at her and nodded.

"About a year later our families took us to a travelling circus independently. We bumped into each other and found out we lived only about three fields away from each other, as the crow flies, so we started meeting up to play.

Initially we'd play hide and seek in the local woods but gradually as we got a little older, we both started to feel something stronger between us. Outwardly to our parents we just seemed like close friends, but she was blossoming into a fine young lady just as I left school and began working in Horncastle in the hardware shop.

A Ghostly Diversion

I reckon both our parents started to suspect there was something closer between us, but we'd become such a part of each other's family that I think they were all happy that we were growing together and almost inseparable. She was there for me when my father was killed in an accident when a tall crane on the building site he was working on toppled over crushing him. Jen got me through it, I'll never forget."

Richard shook his head as more memories came back, and a tear welled up in his right eye. Sally leaned forward and asked in a low, quiet voice.

"In your own time Richard."

He looked at her, nodded and continued.

"When I was about to leave school, we'd stumbled upon an old tunnel starting in the woods not far from her place that was probably once part of the old manor. Very messy, but for us at the time it was like discovering a new planet or a lost Pharaoh's tomb. We couldn't believe no one seemed to know anything about it so we kept shtum, it was our secret hideaway.

I didn't have many friends you see - even those who seemed friendly always took the piss out of my friendship *with a girl*. Guess they were the immature ones after all. It was only when they were older that the likes of Marcus, Fred and Charles start to appreciate what I and Jenny felt long before they did.

As for the tunnel I never told the lads about it. You couldn't go far into it at first but getting the job at the hardware store was perfect and without Jenny initially knowing, I secretly cleaned out the rest of the tunnel. Mind you I didn't realise just how far back it went - felt like bloody miles I can tell you. Anyway, I sorted it that the entrance would be difficult to find, the tree roots doing most of the work to hide the opening, so our secret hideaway wouldn't be found. Not that there were many others of our age roaming the area as it was supposed to be haunted by all accounts by that old Frenchie chap of the manor, but I didn't want to take any chances. Still can't believe it's stayed undiscovered until today.

When it was ready, I took Jenny into it and she loved it, thrilled to bits and of course with me. As she began to blossom it gradually became our little love nest. We didn't do anything wrong at first, just sort o' laid there next to each other like and cuddled… but eventually, well you can imagine our feelings would start to take over.

You can guess that even her parents and my mother would not have been impressed if they'd found out we'd started having sex and I'm sure I don't need to tell you how much trouble we'd be in legally due to her age. We didn't care though, that's love I guess."

He paused and took a sip of water but for several moments just stared into the distance. Sally was still holding his hand and squeezed it gently.

"What happened on the day she disappeared Richard?"

He hesitated and sighed, looked aimlessly around the room and then at Mike and Sally in turn.

"Jack and Barbara went into Lincoln to do the weekly shop and Jenny and I had arranged to meet up at her place that afternoon."

Memories flooded back again as he recounted the fateful day's events…

19: That fateful day…

"Yes Mom, I'll be all right." Jenny smiled at her mother across the table and cocked her head to one side. "Richard's coming over, he's got a posh bike now and he wants to show off, you know how he is." Barbara smiled back at Jenny but with a wry look on her face at the same time.

"Now you know we love Richard and it's clear you two are very close but promise me… nothing, you know, nothing…" She hesitated.

*"Aww MOM, YUK, come on, you know I wouldn't do **'that'**, well not yet anyway!" She giggled and Barbara batted her lightly over the head with the Daily Mirror.*

"If you want to talk about 'it' then I'm here for you love but I don't want you making any mistakes so early in your life. Not like Chloe's daughter - huh, the slut."

Jenny looked at her mum in mock disgust then smiled.

"Mom, she was stupid, I'm not, so there. Richard is really sweet, and you know he's such a gentleman. He has to ask just to kiss me on the cheek!" She leaned across the table again and motioned her mum to move closer as she whispered. "I reckon he's too nervous about that sort of thing anyway. He got all red faced the other week when we were out for a walk and couldn't stop apologising when a gust of wind blew me dress up and he saw me knickers and I…"

"JENNY - you didn't tell me that!"

"Sorry, it was nothing really. At least I was wearing some - not like Chloe's daughter! You did wonder why I was laughing so much when I got back, and I said

A Ghostly Diversion

Richard had tripped on the smallest twig. Sorry for the little lie, it was a white one, promise!"

She looked sheepishly at her mum and Barbara shook her head and smiled just as Jack put his head round the door and looked at each of them in turn. He smiled at Barbara.

"You coming love? I've been waiting like a lump now for a good ten minutes! It's all petrol wasted you know - can't afford to waste it like water now it's over four shillings a gallon. Remember, we're not made of money!" He looked over at Jenny, "You okay poppet?" He asked.

She nodded.

"Yes Dad." She smiled warmly back at him. Jack left the door open as he went back to their Ford Anglia. Barbara looked straight into Jenny's eyes.

"Right, OK Jenny. I believe you. I'll see you when we get back. We'll bring fish 'n' chips for tea so have the table laid. I'm sure if Richard wants some he can stay for tea as well. I'll make sure we get enough for all of us." Barbara came round and kissed Jenny on her forehead. "Be a good girl, I mean it." She wagged a finger in a joking sort of way. "Don't do anything I wouldn't do, all right?" She said as she went out, closing the door behind her.

Jenny walked over and waved at them from the kitchen window as they drove off then dashed upstairs to her room, started undressing and put her newest and favourite blue low-cut top and her favourite summer flowers skirt on. She tidied her hair, made sure her hair clip was in place then looked out the window expectantly. No sign of Richard yet so she sat down on her bed, got back up and walked over to her mirror and checked she was presentable, adjusted her new bra for the umpteenth time and appraised her figure.

Suddenly she heard a bicycle bell tinkle, her eyes lit up as she glanced out the window and dashed back

A Ghostly Diversion

downstairs just in time to fling the door open as Richard was about to knock.

"Wow, you psychic or what?" He exclaimed as she wrapped her arms around him and planted a big kiss on his lips. "That confirms you've missed me then." He pulled her back to him and kissed her again whilst caressing her behind. She pushed his hands away but kept hold of them. Then put them back with a grin on her face.

"Later." She teased.

He grinned back at her.

"How long's yer parents away for then?"

"All afternoon. What we gonna do, go for a waaalk?" She asked, knowing full well what they really would probably get up to. Then she had a thought. "Oooo can I have a ride on your new bike?" She asked in an excited rising tone, and he shrugged.

"Could do. Have anywhere in particular in mind?" He asked fully knowing what she really wanted him to say. She put her arms on her hips, pouted her lips, and stepped back from him.

"Stop teasing. You've been working all week and I've missed you; I've had to put up with school!" She said raising her eyebrows and he looked at her cocking his head to one side.

"Oh I get it - just want me for one thing, apart from my witty banter, the money I earn now, my..." She rushed at him and planted another kiss on his lips. He didn't resist. After a few moments she let go and he stepped back and took a good appreciative look at her for which she did a twirl.

That allowed the skirt to fly up and Richard whistled in approval. He pulled her back close to him then looked down and smiled.

"You getting bigger or what?" He enquired teasingly.

A Ghostly Diversion

Jenny grinned up at him.

"Mom treated me to a new bra when she got back from Nottingham on Wednesday. Do ya like it" And she whipped her top quickly up and down making Richard again whistle softly. "I think that's a yes" She beamed at him and then a more serious look came over her.

"You know we're going to have to be more careful. I'm pretty sure that Mom also noticed I'd got the new bra on, and she knows we're meeting up this afternoon. She didn't see me in this top or the skirt though. I daren't let on what we've been up to, she'd shoot me, not to mention what Dad would do and you'd be in a lot of trouble."

"ME be more careful, you're the one that makes a show of things! More than that - it's all right for you but I'm the one who could be arrested!"

He held her close to him again. "But I love you and it's worth the chances we take."

Jenny nestled into his chest.

"I know - I love you too."

She lightened up again "Come on - fancy that walk?" She looked at him with a mischievous glance as they held hands and went out the door, only for Jenny to stop, let go of his hand and rush back inside. She looked round and spotted her mother's notepad on the table next to the vase. Quickly she jotted down a couple of lines on it before taking it to the back door and pinning it up on the outside.

She hesitated then dashed back indoors and grabbed her purse from the mantelpiece before leaving then locked the door with her key. Richard looked at the note and read:

Mom/Dad,

A Ghostly Diversion

Rich is late and so I'm off down the road to meet up with him. See ya later.
Luv ya.
Poppet!

Jenny shrugged at Richard.

"Best to cover us in case they come back early." They again held hands and began walking round to the front of 'Wolds View' cottage along the concrete slab path and onto the road verge. She looked back at the cottage and seemed puzzled.

"Where's ya bike then?" Richard nodded towards the side of the wooden shed her dad used as a makeshift garage, then she spotted it. "Ooo looks nice even from here, can I have a ride then?" She asked quite innocently, and Richard guffawed then regained his composure.

"I'm sure you'll enjoy it, 'and' the bike." He added and with that saucy comment Jenny slapped him playfully on the backside, but Richard stopped suddenly and pulled her into a gap in the hedge at the roadside. He hushed his voice and motioned to her. "Just stay down for a moment. I can see Marcus, Fred and Charlie coming up the road on their bikes. They'll make life hell for us if they see us together."

"I could put them off by flashing my top at them if you like."

Richard shushed her quickly and they kept low, hidden behind the hedge. Jenny tried to stifle a giggle and playfully tried to grope Richard, but he hushed her again looking quite serious this time. The three lads merrily rode past throwing insults at each other as they carried on their way laughing at the rude words they'd used, thinking no one could hear them.

A Ghostly Diversion

A few moments later they passed the cottage and a little further on rounded a slight bend in the road, lost to sight and Richard gave out a sigh of relief. They both got up and carried on walking but soon came to a small animal made path. It cut through another gap in the hedge and tree line and heading off across the field roughly towards the smaller wood across from them to the north.

Richard went to walk onto the path, but Jenny couldn't wait and rushed off along it. Richard quickly followed and caught up with her, patting her on her behind and racing ahead of her in a bust of speed. Jenny laughed and rushed after him. She caught him up just as they got to a wooden bridge crossing the ditch with the woods just past it.

For a moment they stopped, made their way carefully over it knowing it was already showing signs of collapsing, then they embraced again, and Jenny gave him a quick kiss on the cheek.

Suddenly she grabbed his crotch, squeezing lightly and raced away along the ditch bank screaming in laughter as she knew what would come next. Richard partially buckled from the shock and surprise of her grip then bolted after her. Grabbing her from behind they almost toppled into the ditch but regained their feet as they playfully wrestled along the ditch bank top.

Richard grabbed Jenny and got her into a headlock with his arm lightly around her neck and began playfully scuffling her hair, almost dislodging the tiny black plastic hair clip. She shouted half for fun and half annoyed at the thought of losing the clip but then everything happened in a flash.

Jenny's foot slid on a smooth stone jutting out from the side of the ditch near to the top. She slipped, gave out a panicked scream and fell down the side of the bank dragging Richard with her. He tried to pull her back instinctively but without comprehending he was still holding her in a headlock and, as they both slid down, her neck gave out an awful crack.

Jenny began convulsing, gurgling, and twitching as they both came to a stop at the bottom of the ditch in a small trickle of water as Richard screamed Jenny's name over and over again. She stopped convulsing with her eyes bulging, wide open staring up at him lying there partially on top of him, dead.

He began shaking and stammering to himself calling her name repeatedly, gently rocking her for several minutes, beginning to sob as he turned her over and cradled her in his arms as the inevitable truth of the situation dawned on him…

20: The missing…

"Now we have to be clear on this point Richard, are you willing to stand up in court and repeat all of this under oath, say that is what happened on that day and ask us to believe that it was simply an accident?" asked Sally.

Richard had tears in his eyes, it was clear that he was a broken man having kept that terrible event to himself for all these years. Sally passed him a tissue from a pack near the table edge. He took another sip of water and stared into the glass.

"Yes detective, I've nothing to lose, it's over. She meant the world to me. There's never been anyone like Jenny since and never will be."

Mike now leaned forward.

"So, what happened after you both fell? Why didn't you fetch help? Why did you take her body into the woods to hide her?"

Richard shook his head.

"She was dead, I felt for her pulse and there was nothing. I realised it would all look wrong, and I began to panic. It was then that I came to a stupid decision, something that instead of going for help, I can never go back on…"

He resumed where he'd left off.

#

For a few minutes Richard sat with Jenny checking for a pulse and sobbing but the water from the drain was seeping into his trousers and making him cold and he knew something had to be done. They couldn't stay where they were. He didn't know how long Jenny's parents would really be away for and he couldn't be seen with her body. He calmed himself down and started to think of what to do. A practical, firm, but ultimately cold-hearted feeling came over him as he realised that with Jenny being underage any post-mortem would quickly discover she was no longer a virgin, and he knew that all fingers would point (in truth) at himself.

He braced himself, closed her eyelids, carefully lifted Jenny's body onto his shoulder and managed to scramble up the side of the ditch being careful to check to see if there was anyone about over near the road. He was on the north side and quickly he found their usual route into the woods. Taking her lifeless body off his shoulders he carried her in his arms into the wood and out of anyone's possible view.

He hesitated, then a thought struck him. He located the hidden entrance to their tunnel and put her down to push past the stiff tree roots and open the small wooden door he'd fashioned. Carefully, Richard managed to pull Jenny into the tunnel and out of sight. Using the torches, he'd set up along the line of it during happier times, he was able to carry her down a few small steps and the tunnel was then high enough for him to carry her in his arms to their love nest.

He'd worked hard in the months before to make it comfortable with layers of blankets and several cushions and for a moment he thought back to the lovemaking they'd done here. He shook his head, lay her down carefully and wrapped one of the blankets round her. As he did so he noticed Jenny's cheap but favourite hair clip had dropped onto the cushion.

Without a moment's hesitation he picked it up and put it in his pocket. Tears welled up in his eyes and he sobbed again seeing her there lifeless and wishing he could turn the clock back.

A Ghostly Diversion

"I'm sorry, sweetheart, I'm so, so sorry." He hugged her lifeless form for what seemed like ages. A sudden though occurred to him as he looked at her now dishevelled clothes, her parents would find the clothes she said she was wearing when they last saw her, they would be in her bedroom. He carefully searched in Jenny's purse and found the door key. He nervously headed back, entered the cottage and ran up to Jenny's bedroom. He'd only been up in her room once and they'd nearly been caught but now he was in a panic, located the top and skirt Jenny had mentioned to him earlier and, tucking them under his arm, he retraced his steps, locked the house up before carefully heading back unseen to the woods.

Once again, he sat with her lifeless body, placing the bundle of clothes next to her, and cried again for several minutes before he finally calmed down enough to leave. He made his way back to the entrance turning the torches off one by one as he did so. He looked outside and satisfied there was no one around he carefully emerged, placed the door back and moved the camouflage netting and tree roots back in place to hide the entrance.

Stepping back, he noticed a few footprints and almost panicked but then got a branch and managed to disturb the ground until they too could not be seen. He knew his hands were dirty and he reckoned he'd wiped his face probably dirtying that as well but a little further on near the edge of the wood he knew there was another small stream. It was the original course of the water before the ditch was added as extra drainage.

He found and carefully washed in a shallow pool as best he could. Looking in the water he reckoned he was clean enough and then headed slowly back to the other edge of the woods keeping an eye out just in case anyone was out for a walk.

A Ghostly Diversion

Looking about to see if he could spot anyone, he made his way back to where they'd slipped and managed to clear what few signs there were of where they'd slipped down the ditch side. Back over the bridge he set off retracing their original path and route back to 'Wolds View' and picking up his bike, made his way home being careful not to be seen.

#

"Ok - so you've hidden the body and covered your physical tracks, but your mother must have known something was wrong and covered for you. She was the one who could, and did, back up your alibi."

Sally pointed out as she looked over the original statements made at the time of Jenny's disappearance that Mike had slid across to her.

Richard nodded slowly.

"When I got home Mum was surprised, I was back early - she'd figured what me and Jenny were up to and had warned me to be extra careful. She herself loved Jenny and I reckon she was looking forward to having grandchildren, but I couldn't keep it from her, and I confessed everything. She flew into a rage for a few minutes before sitting down heavily on the kitchen chair and putting her head in her hands.

It was she who decided on the alibi as mum was determined not to see me go to prison. She had an idea, sat me down and we went over and over what I was to say until I was exhausted. By then Jenny's parents had got home and all they knew was that her note said she was taking a walk down to meet up with me.

A Ghostly Diversion

It was only natural they'd suspect me so mum was set on making sure I could get through any interrogation. In fact, you, Mr Freshman, was the young copper at the time who came with the detective to oversee the questioning."

Mike looked at him and nodded.

"Yes - I was literally a 'freshman' at it and I was taken in by your story although I was a little naïve myself but felt something was not right. I was a young copper and knew I wouldn't be listened to, more's the pity." Mike had noticed all the while whilst Richard had been making his confession, he'd been fumbling with a small locket he'd fished out of his jacket pocket near the start of his confession.

"Tell me - what is that you've got there?"

Mike held out his hand expectantly.

Richard looked down at it and then clicked it open, to reveal a small black plastic hair clip, Jenny's. Sally took an intake of breath then reached under the table into a hold all and fetched out a clear zip lock bag and clear plastic gloves. She put the latter on before reaching over and taking the hair clip off Richard, placing it in the bag for later analysis and as evidence. She also looked at Mike with this development, but he just nodded and remained professional as he gazed intently towards Richard.

He leaned forward and looked Dreyer in the eyes.

"But we did a thorough search of the woods with the villagers…" Mike trailed off as he began to suspect how they'd missed finding the tunnel. Richard looked at him and nodded knowing what Mike was thinking so he continued.

A Ghostly Diversion

"If you remember Jenny wasn't declared missing for a couple of days initially as Barbara and Jack clung to the belief she would turn up. They'd come to my mothers on the evening to find I was laid up in bed with the flu according to what mother told them. Once they began to despair and did contact the police, I'd by then ironically actually gone down with a bad cold. Mum used it to bolster my alibi for why I hadn't met up with Jenny.

When the Police asked the public for help in searching the area the whole village turned out, including me. Despite my cold, I got wrapped up thoroughly and mum and I managed to work our way to a point where I was the one 'checking' the line that passed over where I knew the tunnel entrance was." He shrugged. "It worked - can't say more than that. Nobody suspected a thing. If it had been yerself or another copper, then you might have noticed something but as it was, we got away with it."

Richard looked at each in turn. "I didn't deliberately kill her; it was a genuine accident, but I realise what you have to do and I understand completely."

He lowered his head.

Mike stood up.

"All these years and I always suspected you were involved but you are right. Not murder, probably manslaughter but we'll have to let a court decide what must be done with you." Mike looked at Sally, nodded and left the room leaving her to deal with charging Richard as he went off to find James.

21: Farewell and bad news…

Mike visited James and Helen a week after the confession and pointed out that the coroner would release the body soon for burial but there was the problem of who would pay for the funeral. However, in a surprising development a social media website set up a memorial and donations page for Jennifer Portisham after Helen posted a plea on her page online. The donations came flooding in from around the world as the news media reported on the tragic story.

It had been a long time since Grasceby church had been full. After Richard had come clean about events fifty years earlier and it became public knowledge, there was mixed reaction from the local community. Outright disbelief that an upstanding member of the community could have kept something like Jenny's death quiet all those years, to those who saw events back in 1960 as a tragic accident and a young man who panicked, making yet another tragic mistake by not coming forward at the time.

One thing was sure though. No one knew where Jenny's mother, Barbara Portisham, was and efforts to find her had proved futile both back in 1960 and now. It was even possible she too had passed away in the intervening years, never to know her daughter's fate.

One thing was missing however from the coverage in the media, by his request to Mike and Sally, there was no mention of James seeing her ghost or helping them with their enquiries. James

A Ghostly Diversion

knew that at some point someone might start asking questions as several had worked out why James had been interested in 'Wolds View' cottage. His boss, Mark, agreed to keep it quiet even though he thought it would give the business some publicity as in the end he appreciated the work James did and indeed their long-time friendship.

Meanwhile Craig had also kept quiet and for a while seemed to distance himself from James at work as he'd apparently at last found the love of his life. It was slightly frustrating though that he wouldn't talk about her or even tell James her name, but Craig insisted it was because he didn't want to jinx things as he had always seemed to do with his past relationships.

James himself hoped to keep out of the spotlight and had been concerned about attending the service with burial set for 1:30pm, but something told him deep inside he had to see it through to its natural conclusion, if only for Jennifer's sake. Still the funeral had been a moving, if solemn, occasion with people packing the church, both locals and people just moved by the story as portrayed in the media who, of course, covered it on radio and local TV. James was glad they concentrated on the two detectives, Mike, and Sally for their comments.

Jenny was laid to rest next to her father's grave. With no family present, Mike, Sally, with Richard Dreyer between them but handcuffed to a police officer, James, Helen, and Craig all stood nearby as the coffin was lowered into the grave next to Jennifer's father, Jack. They all took turns throwing a handful of soil on the coffin then stepped

A Ghostly Diversion

back and waited for Reverend Cossant to finish her prayers.

Final prayer done; the Police constable took Dreyer away with his head bowed low as the remaining five began walking back to where their cars were parked. Craig gave his excuses, briefly looked at Helen then strolled on ahead as Mark had only given him enough time off for the actual service and was expecting him back to work straight away.

Mark had been more understanding to James and so he had the afternoon off much to the natural annoyance it seemed of Craig. They walked in silence for a short distance; Sally was the first to speak as they were halfway down the stone path.

"You know one thing puzzles me about today, how did they know there was enough room to add Jenny's body at the grave side. Mr Portisham died relatively young, in his late thirties, so probably wouldn't have been thinking about such a large plot, if he even thought about it at all."

Mike smiled though.

"Actually Barbara, Mrs Portisham, arranged it when they came to bury Jack. I guess she expected to be buried alongside him and I gather from the vicarage, the records showed she arranged for a family plot. I wonder if she'd begun to accept Jenny could be dead and planned accordingly."

"She must have been quite a woman, only daughter vanishes, husband dies only a couple of months or so before their second child is due to be born. Her world was coming apart at the seams. I assume Jack must have known she was pregnant?" asked Helen and Mike nodded positively.

A Ghostly Diversion

"Yes. That to me makes it even more tragic." He said. "I gather there's still money coming into the donations website and there's talk of a marble headstone for the grave. Only fitting really. James? You're quiet, you, OK?".

James looked up from where he'd been listening to them whilst looking at the ground as they walked along the churchyard path past a bench.

"Yeah. Still gets to me though that there was no traceable family to be present, just seems so sad but I guess at least Jenny's story is now over. If you believe in an afterlife or heaven or whatever, at least she's probably up there now with her dad."

He hesitated for a brief moment. "I know I can tell you this, I've been back several times to the cottage, and I've not seen Jenny since her body was found. I hope that means she's finally at peace." They all nodded in agreement at this then Helen felt something in her pocket and brought out her phone. Her expression turned to one of concern and she turned to James.

"James, we need to go. I said to have your phone with you. It's the care home." James looked quickly at her, concerned.

"Mum?"

Helen nodded and showed him the text that had come through. He turned to Mike and Sally. "We'd best get off, Mum's taken a turn for the worse and we've been told to go down to Albury immediately. You two going to the Star and Crescent Moon Inn now? I hear Marcus has put on quite a spread for anyone wishing to go along. But we'd best be going, pass on our apologies to those who know us."

A Ghostly Diversion

Mike and Sally both held James' and Helen's hands and Mike leaned over and kissed Helen on the cheek whilst Sally did likewise with James as she squeezed his hand then let go.

"Hope she's okay and hope to see you both soon, let us know when you're back home." Said Sally as they reached her car in which she was giving Mike a lift to the Inn. They got in and drove off as Helen's phone once again rang, this time with a call. She noted the caller id and looked apprehensive, then gave the phone to James. He listened to the call as they too finally reached their car.

"Thank you for letting us know, I understand, my fault but ironically we've been at a funeral today and just come out. Yes, yes, we'll be down, I expect we'll get there around eight if the traffic isn't too bad. Yes, okay, you did what you could, and we really appreciate it. Yes, thank you."

Helen's hand went to his free arm and gently squeezed it as he turned to her ashen faced with a lost look in his eye.

"Mums died" he said quietly.

#

The inn was quite full considering only a few old enough to remember the Portishams, were left.

"There was no doubting it, they were in love." Fred said as he sipped his pint and took a sandwich from the tray offered by the barmaid, Sharon.

Mike and Sally had barely got in through the inn door when he'd cornered them insisting they join the small group at the table.

A Ghostly Diversion

"Yes, I know" said Mike, "You even made that clear when I tried to reopen the case thirty years ago but now at least we know the truth. Shame Richard didn't come clean in the first place though. Would've saved more hassle."

Sally looked at them and at Charles and Marcus across the table.

"How come no one knew about the Manor or the tunnel though - surely some historian should have come up with something that indicated there was one."

Charles leaned across.

"Well, I've been working for the estate all my life and I thought I knew every scrap of their land but I didn't even know there'd been a former manor. History wasn't my thing. Twasn't until that James chappie contacted the local archaeological society about it that I found out. The estate wasn't too keen initially on having their land dug up on what could have been a fool's errand. For Richard to find the tunnel, do what he did *and* keep summat like that to himself all these years…" He shook his head. "Must have been awful knowing that there was always a chance someone else might find it."

Mike looked thoughtful.

"From what James discovered, apparently the tunnel extended from the location of the old kitchen, due south away from the manor. It would only have been used by the servants and kitchen staff to take any waste down and dump it in the ditch. Rain would have then washed it away for them. That's why it could take a person standing up.

No one could have known it had survived - heck there is so little about the original manor left that I'm amazed James found anything at all! Well, it's over and done with now, case is closed, eh Sally?" He looked at his younger colleague and she nodded.

"Pretty much so. Once they found a few small items associated with Mr Dreyer, such as the torches plus the DNA samples that confirmed he'd been there, then the rest fell into place. It's now down to how the judge interprets the mass of evidence.

Off the record, Mr Dreyer's main crime is actually withholding vital evidence all these years and misleading the original investigation. He might get manslaughter under diminished responsibility if he's lucky and the judge believes his side of the story.

The coroner has confirmed the post-mortem didn't show any signs of a violent struggle, only possible marks round the neck which can be characteristic of someone in a head hold so it seems Mr Dreyer's account could be true. But without actually travelling back in time we'll probably never know for sure." She looked into her glass of orange juice thoughtfully.

Mike looked at her briefly as if about to add that James had seen 'everything' but held back knowing it took them into a bit of a bitter divide between himself and his younger colleague.

Fred piped up.

"Yes, saw that in this morning's paper before I came out for the funeral. Anyhow where's that James and his missus anyway?" Fred turned to Mike. "Seemed like you two had become good buddies if you ask me." Mike put his pint down, but Sally interjected.

A Ghostly Diversion

"Him and Helen have had some bad news, apparently his mum has been taken very ill and they're off down to see her somewhere on the outskirts of London as we speak."

"Well, I hope everything's all right. Anyhow, must go. Got to check on the cattle, you coming Charles?" asked Fred and they gave their excuses along with Marcus who was called back to the bar. Sharon was getting a little irate at having to serve so many people without her dad to help.

As they were now alone on their table Sally turned to Mike with a questioning look on her face.

"I'm intrigued. I can't say I believe in ghosts but when I compared Richard's confession with the account James gave of what he thought he'd seen and interpreted I have to say they were remarkably similar. Indeed, if it wasn't for the fact that James wasn't alive at the time of Jenny's death, and I'd been in your shoes, I'd have *had* to have brought James in for questioning."

Mike looked at her thoughtfully.

"I thought the very same thing. It was the little details that were uncanny for me. The hair clip was slightly chilling as I made clear to you both it wasn't made public at the time, and I've never found any public reference to it in the news media. The only reference was in my personal notes of the case. Even old GH didn't make a note of it in his official report at the time." He looked at her as she seemed lost in her own thoughts. She seemed to realise this and turned to him.

"Why James? Why not someone else? There must have been others who've passed that place, I mean - there was that young couple I suppose, who fled the cottage after renting it and the estate assistant may have seen something - but he died so I guess we'll never know." Mike leaned into her and lowered his voice.

"Firstly, there *were* other sightings but nothing you'd have put money on. Especially Marcus over there. He was in his early twenties and was cycling past the house when he claimed he saw Jenny walking along the roadside near her house. He rode up to her where she suddenly vanished, apparently, he fell off his bike in shock. Trouble was no one took him seriously as he was also drunk at the time. I gather it's a miracle he even made it home by all accounts.

What's more he described Jenny's clothes exactly as James did which of course in the official report she was wearing the clothes her mum had last seen her in. Little did she know that Jenny changed into something else for Richard. That was the other thing that really intrigued me about James description of Jenny. It didn't match the official account, but it did match Marcus's account of seeing her ghost."

Sally looked thoughtful.

"Poor James, hope his mum is OK. Did you notice the, err, looks between Craig and Helen?"

"Listen," he leaned slightly to her and dropped his voice a little. "I know you're now divorced but you seem a little, shall we say, taken with James. Helen's a good woman Sally and I'm sure I'm not the only one who's seen the look you have when you're talking with and about him. I'm sure there's nothing between Craig and Helen, they're just good friends that's all. So, leave it be."

A Ghostly Diversion

He touched her arm gently. She grimaced at him but didn't say any more, just nodded. However, her female instincts along with her investigative training were telling her something else.

A Ghostly Diversion

#

The on-duty care staff recognised them as they came through the doors and greeted them apologetically.

"I'm really sorry we had to contact you in the way we did but there was no answer from your home line and Mr Hansone your mobile phone appeared to be turned off." Kerry lowered her head with respect as she said this.

"That's alright - you did the right thing; it was my fault not yours. Was it...was it quick and painless?" James felt he knew the answer but needed to know.

"It seems so. She'd been pretty much out of it for the last few days, barely eating and sleeping most of the time day and night. She did come round for a short while at lunchtime and pointed at the TV screen a couple of times but by then we couldn't make any sense out of her except the word 'home' - not even sure what was on at the time, so we think she was becoming delirious. At about one thirty this afternoon she slipped away in her sleep. I'm so sorry."

Kerry took them into a separate room adjacent to the main care home where the recently deceased could be prepared and family could pay their respects. "We'll need a few signatures I'm afraid, but you can do that after you've had some time with her. I'll leave you in peace now.

Press this button on the wall there if you need anything. I'm really sorry for your loss and if it's any consolation she did mention you in her more lucid moments; she was very proud of you both."

A Ghostly Diversion

James and Helen nodded, and Kerry left the room as they sat down next to the bed and James held his mother's hand for the last time.

22: Of changing hearts…

It had been a difficult few weeks. His mother's funeral over and her cottage, his old family home, put on the market, James and Helen brought back over a dozen boxes of keepsakes. Most were old diaries and family photos of him growing up, former girlfriends (much to Helen's amusement) and then with Helen, their courtship, marriage and some of their holiday shots they'd given her. There was plenty to sort through, but for both, work came first, and the boxes were put on one side next to the drinks cabinet to be dealt with later.

Over the next couple of months though it became increasingly clear to James that things were not right with Helen. She seemed to be too eager to get off to her 'classes', 'village meetings' and the like. It didn't take long for him to realise he had lost her, not just to anyone but to his former friend Craig. James was still reeling from the loss of his mother and despite everything he and Helen had been through together she seemed to have become cold when around him.

Although hurtful it came as no surprise when Craig announced he was leaving, not just the company, but also moving away to Nottingham to be closer to his relatives. Helen confirmed James's worst fears when she decided to move with Craig and asked for a divorce, citing unreasonable behaviour - a.k.a. James's pursuit of the truth about the ghostly Jenny. By now though James realised he would be better off not contesting it and, as proceedings took their course, he was grateful that he was able to keep the house by buying Helen's share out with the inheritance from the sale of his mother's house.

There would be a few lean months ahead, but he resigned himself to it and buried his head in his work. At least he was going to get paid for giving his talk at the Lincoln Archaeological Society about the old 'De Grasceby' manor and in fact he'd had several more requests from the East Midlands area groups, so perhaps it would take his mind off things.

In the meantime, James ignored several phone calls from Sally, after Mike had intimated, she was interested in him, until one day she phoned saying it was police business.

She turned up on his doorstep and he let her in puzzled at why she needed to ask him more questions about the Portisham case. The official missing persons case was now closed once Jenny had been buried although he half suspected it was probably more to do with Richard Dreyer. He'd noticed that recent news reports indicated there was a rumour he was going to appeal if he was convicted and sent to prison.

Sally sat down in the single chair across from the sofa and looked at least in an official mood even if she was dressed more for a day out rather than on police business.

"I've called several times James, I heard about Helen and Craig, pretty awful if you ask me and yet she seemed lovely when I first met her."

James sat on the sofa and frowned at her. "I thought this was an official visit?" He tried not to glance at her legs though. She noticed his attention and nodded.

"It is... and isn't."

A Ghostly Diversion

Sally looked at him hesitantly to see what his reaction was, but he didn't show any emotion. "In my official capacity I'm still putting the final touches to the case regarding Dreyer but there's been one thing really getting to me since we first met. Why you?"

She looked at him quizzically, expecting an answer.

"Why me what?" He looked back at her suspiciously wondering if he'd done anything illegal - apart from trespassing on private property of course!

"Jenny. Appear to you of all people? You're an outsider, you hadn't been here long yet for some reason you were the one she chose. Or did she? Blind luck or chance? I'm still trying to get my head around it." She leaned back and crossed her arms across her chest.

"Considering you were sceptical, I thought you didn't believe in ghosts so why change your tune now?" He replied.

She smiled back at him noting he'd leaned forward towards her.

"When I'm working, I can't let such things get in the way of good detective work. But off duty on the other hand, I keep a more open mind. As per today."

"Hang on - you said this was official!" He narrowed his eyes but couldn't help relaxing in her presence and realised he was pleased she was there.

Sally braced herself but she was here now and time to come clean.

"A little white lie. I am off duty but did have a couple of questions, I've also just been wanting to see how you are. Is that really a crime? If so, then I'd best arrest myself I guess!"

James looked at her, smiled and raised his eyebrows.

"You tell me, you're the law aren't you! It's been a hard few months since mum died and then Helen cheating on me of course." He sat back in the chair and felt himself begin to relax, for the first time in what seemed like ages.

"Sorry. I haven't really felt like being in touch with anyone. Haven't even spoken to Mike recently. Is he OK? I bet he enjoyed helping get to the bottom of Jenny's disappearance. I guess it was like closure for him after all those years wondering what had become of her. As for work, it's OK now that Craig has left - that b'st'd! As for why Jenny seemed to choose me - I haven't a clue, really I haven't."

Sally cocked her head to one side. "So, what made you take such an out of the way route then as it's an odd way to go to Lincoln. Don't you work on the outskirts on the new bypass industrial estate?"

He leaned back in his chair and thought back to how it all started. He'd not actually thought about the diversion in a long time. Once the roadworks had finished, they seemed to be a distant memory considering what had happened in the meantime.

"Remember early last summer when there was all those roadworks on the A158 past Baumber? Well one morning I was stuck in, what the radio announcer stated, was a four-mile tail back and on the spur of the moment I took a left turn. Mind you, come to think of it - that's when I first saw Dreyer's

A Ghostly Diversion

dark blue metallic Mercedes. I'd almost forgotten about that.

Well, he took the turning and when I got to it, I suddenly found myself taking it as well. Quite a diversion that turned out to be. I seem to remember that as I passed 'Wolds View' I didn't see it the first time, but I did get a strange chill; at the time I didn't think anything of it. That first time I didn't even notice the cottage as it was set back from the road.

It was only when I started using the route on a semi regular basis to avoid the roadworks that I spotted 'Wolds View' and began to see Jenny at the upper left-hand window. The rest, well I guess that's history."

"So, you could say we've met because of *'a ghostly diversion'*" She made the last words seem all spooky as she waved her hands around in the air and he smiled, she could be quite funny really, he thought.

"Very funny, but I suppose in a way you could say that." He got up noting the time and he had things to do he told himself. "Anyway, anything else detective?" He managed to make the last question sound as if he was toying with her, but she just shook her head, smiled and got up. James opened the door but as Sally stepped out, she half turned and put her hand on his arm.

"James, you have my number. I know it's perhaps too early but if you really need a shoulder then please, do call me. Remember I've been through this the other year. I just wished I'd talked to someone at the time and got things off my chest. OK?"

A Ghostly Diversion

He smiled and kissed her lightly on the cheek noting she had quite a nice chest. He quickly focused back on her eyes.

"OK, and thanks for coming, it does help..." Sally smiled at him, nodded and walked down the driveway to her car. As she drove off, she smiled again and waved at him and, for the first time in many months, James felt good inside.

\#

A few days later James was glad the week was over but now Friday afternoon was here he wished he hadn't taken the afternoon off work when Mark had offered it. Mark wasn't usually that generous so on the spur of the moment James had accepted, but now the house seemed empty when he got in.

Since Helen had taken most of what she considered 'her' belongings, some of the furniture had gone and the rooms looked a little sparse, although he knew there would be some things, she'd still be asking him to return.

He threw together some sandwiches and flopped down on the sofa with a glass of pear cider, for good measure, as he tucked into them. He nodded off to sleep but was awakened with a start when the front doorbell chimed. Opening it he was faced with Helen standing with crossed arms, whilst down at the entrance to the drive he could just make out the back end of Craig's car. He couldn't see the sod himself.

"What do you want?" He snapped at her. Helen lowered her head and pursed her lips.

A Ghostly Diversion

"I, erm, I've got a couple of boxes left in the spare room and I'd like to take them now if it's no trouble." She looked at him with an almost caring look if that were at all possible considering the circumstances.

"Be quick about it as I've got friends coming round, you know, people who I can actually trust!" He answered sarcastically knowing full well he had no such plans. Helen flinched slightly and hurried past him as she rushed upstairs and rummaged around. She didn't take long, and they were indeed the boxes he remembered she'd left. He'd thought about putting them in the bin but knew he wasn't really the vindictive type. Helen stepped past him and started to leave then half turned back to face him as she peered over the top of the boxes.

"I am sorry, you know, it wasn't planned, it just happened." She looked down at her feet as best she could. "Look after yourself, won't you?"

James just nodded as she hurried down the driveway and out of sight. James stood for a moment hearing the car drive off, then he went back inside and flopped once more onto the sofa. Half an hour passed by, then a resolve came over him and he clicked through his contacts on the phone.

Quickly finding the number, he waited for it to connect but after several attempts Sally didn't respond. Feeling somewhat foolish, he was just putting it down when a text message came through instead: *'at work but free to have a quick chat in ten minutes. Sally'*. James smiled and for the first time for a few days he inwardly relaxed and felt good.

Before he could call back after the time had elapsed the phone chimed, he picked it up eagerly spotting who the caller was.

"Hi James, you want me for something?" Sally's voice was refreshing to his ears. He hesitated for a second.

"I was wondering - it would be good to have a chat and I'm not doing anything this weekend so do you want to come over? Err…" He hesitated as he realised how that sounded. "I mean by all means come over sometime over the weekend, it's not a *date* you understand, it's… it's…well I could do with some company and like…" He trailed off realising he sounded weak, pathetic and worse, more like a wimp.

Sally didn't hesitate to reply though.

"I'd love to. Tell you what, I finish at six tonight and I am free for the weekend so, well…you've got a spare room haven't you? Perhaps I can stay over, and we can talk as much as you want. If that's not too presumptuous on my part that is…"

If they'd switched to video mode it would have been obvious to each other that they were grinning like proverbial Cheshire cats but both slightly red faced at the same time. He agreed and she ended the call leaving him happier than an hour earlier.

#

Later that evening after their meal they sat on the sofa slightly apart at first and started chatting about their respective pasts. James fetched a couple of glasses, and it didn't take long before they had polished off a bottle of a tasty house white that James couldn't even remember buying, perhaps it was Helen's - tough, too late now he reflected. They'd also sidled closer to each other without realising it. He fetched another bottle and opened it and she didn't object when he filled both their glasses again.

Sally talked about how she'd met her ex, Stephan, in Antwerp at a European Police Federation conference. Fell in love, married quite quickly and they were together in a manner of speaking for twelve years. Like a lot of long-distance relationships, however, their different work shifts and determination to continue working in their own countries meant there was precious little time for each other and just the previous year they'd realised it was over.

It didn't help that not long after her divorce came through it transpired that Stephan had a mistress in Brussels whom he'd been seeing for several years, hence Sally was somewhat bitter about the whole affair. She'd thrown herself into her work as you do and managed to put everything into perspective. She was just grateful they didn't have children and she was surprised to discover that James and Helen were also childless. James didn't want to discuss it though and the subject was quickly dropped.

They talked long into the night and eventually at nearly 3 a.m. they stumbled upstairs. James managed to find sheets and blankets for the spare bed and passed them to Sally. He looked at her but just couldn't say the words, it was still too soon.

She nodded, closing the door behind him and he walked somewhat unsteadily towards his room and managed to open the door pausing for a few moments to let the walls stop spinning. As he stepped in, he half turned hearing the floorboards softly creak behind him. Sally stood there in shocking pink pyjamas behind him, grinning. They bundled into the room and fell onto the bed laughing, somewhat drunk, trying to wrestle with each other's garments…

A Ghostly Diversion

23: Reunion...

The sound was unfamiliar in recent memory. Certainly, the smell was good as he opened his eyes, then shut them quickly as his head decided to spin whilst the sunlight slipped in through a small gap in the curtains. He opened his eyes again and the previous night, or at least part of it, came back to him, especially when he saw an unfamiliar set of pink pyjamas flung on the floor.

He lifted the sheets realising he was naked then realised what it was that had woken him. Someone was cooking bacon! Before he could get up, he heard footsteps running up the stairs and Sally's face popped round the door. Then seeing he was still in bed she came in. He couldn't help but notice she'd only got her panties and blouse on, there was no wonder he beamed a smile back at her.

"Morning, hope you don't mind but I thought a couple of bacon butties would be just the thing, I'm ravenous!" She popped back onto the landing and came back in with them on two plates plus cups of coffee, all on a tray he'd forgotten even owning. She sat down at the side of the bed next to him as he shuffled up into a sitting position and she slid the tray between them.

"We, err, we..." he looked around not quite knowing how or what to ask. She smiled at him though and started shaking her head.

"No, at least I don't think so - too much wine as I reckon, we both went spark out! Look James, there's no rush. I don't mind if we're careful and take it slow, I do care about you. I do think the wine nearly caused us to do something stupid perhaps, but I feel good about us, and I don't want us to spoil things."

He nodded and smiled at her and she continued. "When we've dressed do you fancy a walk? It's a lovely day and it would be nice just to talk and walk without any strings attached."

James smiled, nodded and tucked into the butties with pleasure, a renewed interest in life and, dare he think it, someone to share it with suddenly felt very appealing.

They spent the rest of the morning at a local nature reserve, called in at the Star and Crescent Moon inn for a spot of lunch, being joined for a while by Mike Freshman until he realised, he was probably in the way. The ways of a detective never leave you thought James as he watched Mike realise he was playing gooseberry and gave his excuses leaving them to their meals.

Marcus seemed to have become more friendly to them since he'd discovered the truth about his best friend's past and made sure they had the best service. It was clear though that he was deliberately avoiding asking where Helen was, he'd spotted Craig and Helen together several times before even James knew and had suspected what was going on. As he was often fond of telling his daughter, Sharon, "Tis none of me business what the guests get up to as long as they pay the bill at the end!"

James and Sally left the inn, arm in arm and before returning to James' home early in the afternoon they called in at the local superstore to pick up more groceries and of course restock up on wine.

A Ghostly Diversion

Back at his place, they sat relaxing on the sofa and Sally was enjoying her cup of tea when her curiosity overcame her nervousness as she noticed several boxes by the cabinet.

"What's with the boxes in the corner, next to the drinks cabinet?" she asked as James came to join her on the sofa.

"Well, they're the few boxes of personal papers and diaries of Mum's that I haven't yet sorted through. You know, bits and pieces, old photos and the like. I just haven't felt in the right mood to tackle them since Mum died, then Helen..." His voice faltered and he sighed, sat down and she touched his arm lightly, caressing it thoughtfully.

"You OK? It's been a few months now, but I guess it's still painful?"

"You could say that, although she had reached her nineties so not a bad score really, was it?"

"I didn't think Helen was that old really..."

"Cheeky!" He replied with a grin. He looked at the boxes, then walked over and picked one up and stared at it for a moment. "I thought I'd be doing this with Helen, but..." He looked back at Sally. "Would you mind helping me now?" She smiled and nodded, and he slit the tape holding the top flaps of the box together as he brought it over to the coffee table.

Over the next hour they found themselves laughing at early pictures of James from age 2 until he was a gangly teenager - James winced at that, especially the long hair when he was a fourteen! They found a selection of his and Helen's wedding photos which they quickly consigned to a pile on one side to be forgotten and it wasn't long before they'd gone through three of the boxes. Sally picked the fourth box up and, on opening it, her eyes lit up as she brought out an old music box.

"Oh wow - mum had something like this when I was a kid. Don't know if I've still got it though." She flipped the clasp, lifted the lid and the tinny jingle started up. When fully opened, a little ballerina daintily spun round to the music. James smiled as memories returned of a long forgotten past when he was a child growing up with his mum in Albury.

"Wow - it's a long time since I've heard that. Mum always said it was very special and that I couldn't play with it as it was fragile." He took it from Sally and held it carefully in his hands as his thoughts flew back to a younger time in his life. He held it, mesmerised by the music and watching the ballerina do her whirling until it wound down and stopped.

"Definitely a keepsake, though."

He managed to hold back a tear and went to put it down.

"Aren't you going to look inside then?" Sally asked and he looked at her puzzled. She took it off him and carefully looked it over. "See here, a slight indentation. Didn't you notice that the base is quite deep?" He shook his head as Sally examined it in more detail and James couldn't help but think it was bringing the detective out in her. "A lot of these had a place to keep important things like letters from loved ones or treasured photos and the like."

She stopped as she found what she was looking for and, with a faint 'click', the base showed a crack, and she was able to slide it clear of the musical section. Doing so allowed several items to fall to the floor one of which was a photo laid on the top of several documents and she picked it up and looked at it.

"It's a wedding, looks like it must be your mum and dad at the church they got mar..." Her voice trailed off and her face took on a serious appearance. "That's really odd." She looked at him strangely.

"You'd better take a look at this."

She handed the photo over to him slowly as if not sure that James should look at it. James reached and took it off her and for a moment couldn't see what had got her perturbed like that.

"Why it must be mum and dad's wedding, there she is and..." he also trailed off as he looked at the man, then at the church. "This is not right; no it can't be right. It's Grasceby church and he looks..." James wasn't sure where his voice had gone as the words weren't coming out and his throat had gone dry and felt constricted. Sally was looking at another document and gingerly handed it to him.

He looked in disbelief.

It was a deed poll for someone changing their name and as he looked at the original name and then the new name, shock and a little shiver rippled down his spine. He sat down slowly on the sofa and felt a little lightheaded.

He started to sweat as one by one Sally passed him a couple of birth certificates, a death certificate and some official letters, one of which was from the MOD, he barely took notice of them. Sally motioned to the music box underside.

A Ghostly Diversion

"There's something stuck under it, James" she said quietly and on turning it over he pulled the letter from under the box and read it to himself:

'My dear James,

Naturally if you are reading this, I've either decided to tell you everything or, more likely as I'm weak and old, I've passed on and you are having to go through what few possessions I have got left. I always told you the music box was special and not to be touched and now you are perhaps beginning to realise what I meant and why I didn't want you playing with it lest you discovered the truth too soon.

You have grown up knowing me as Mum or more properly of course as Mrs Mary Catherine Hansone. Let me be clear, I AM your mother. However, you will by now have found the birth certificates and the deed poll. Please, please, please let me explain and please do forgive me for not telling you before, but I was afraid, so very afraid of what your reaction might be.

Many years ago, I changed my name thinking it would protect you. My original married name was Barbara Portisham and your father was Jack Frederick Portisham, not Harry Hansone as I often called him when we talked about him. I always tried to steer the conversation away from him to avoid awkward questions as you were an inquisitive child.

We originally lived in a tiny hamlet called Grasceby in Lincolnshire and we had a daughter many years before you came on the scene. She was called Jennifer and a lovely and fine young lass she was. She had not long turned sixteen, when one Saturday whilst your father and I went shopping in Lincoln, Jenny vanished. There was no trace, her boyfriend and even your father were questioned but Richard, her boyfriend, was a lovely young man and

A Ghostly Diversion

he was just as distraught as we were and just as inconsolable.

We knew he couldn't have done anything to our Jenny as it was clear they were madly in love despite a three-year gap between them in age.

James paused contemplating what his mother would have said and done had she known Richard was the cause of Jenny's disappearance. He leaned back heavily into the sofa, looked back at the letter, took a deep breath and continued reading.

Night and day would go by with no word from her or from the police investigation but after a year I found your father slumped in his chair late one night, dead from heart failure. Doctors even said it themselves when I told them I preferred to think your father was so heartbroken, that he finally gave up hope.

None of us could have possibly known that he actually had a serious heart condition and that it had only been a matter of time. He loved his 'little poppet' as he always called Jenny, and something must have finally given way. Knowing you were on the way I couldn't stay in the cottage any longer after he died, there were too many memories. So, I sold it to the estate and moved to Albury where you were born, and we spent most of your early years growing up there.

When I arrived at our new home just a couple of months before you were born I was able to change my name by deed poll so I could give you a fresh start without being haunted by our tragedy. I know this will be very difficult discovering that I lied to you and that you've grown up not knowing you had a sister somewhere (I never gave up hope!). I kept the faith and always hoped

there would be some news that Jenny had returned but I guess I was wrong to keep all this from you all these years.
> *Please forgive me dearest son.*
> *Your loving mother,*
> *Mary (Barbara Portisham). Mum xx*

The room was silent. James sat perfectly still holding the letter and just staring at it as a tear trickled down his cheek. Sally shuffled over to him and put her arms around him but didn't say a word. He handed the letter to her, and she read it through quietly to herself as she shook her head in disbelief.

After what seemed like an eternity, but was just a few minutes, James coughed, shook his head, wiped away the tears and looked through the other documents that Sally had found. One was the birth certificate for Jennifer Ann Portisham and the death certificate was for his father, Jack. The second birth certificate was for Barbara Conrad, his mother's maiden name.

"I should therefore have been James Anthony Portisham instead of James Anthony Hansone. Jennifer…she was my sister…" and another tear rolled down his left cheek. "My dad…" His voice trailed off as he didn't know what to say or think. Sally held him tightly and he held on to her, lost in his thoughts, as he rocked gently and began to sob for several minutes.

He looked again at the deed poll and shook his head. Then a strange thought occurred to him. He looked through his smart phone contacts until he spotted the one, he was looking for and immediately pressed to call the number. A few moments later he was connected.

A Ghostly Diversion

"Oh, hello, is this reception? Good. A few months back you had been looking after my mother, Mrs Mary Catherine Hansone? Yes, she passed away, yes, yes, that's right the twenty fourth. Yes, I am James Hansone. Err no she's no longer with me, it's a long story. No there's no problem at all with the home, you did a great job and I really appreciated it.

I remember it was Kerry that called me when mum passed away, is she still there? Oh good, is it possible to just have a quick chat with her? Yes, yes I'll hold."

He looked at Sally and she looked at him trying to work out what he was doing. "Mum said something apparently shortly before she died, and I have a suspicion I know what it was she was..." His attention turned back to the phone. "Kerry? I'm fine thank you and, no, no we're no longer together…really long story.

Can you remember when we came up after mum died and you helped us that evening? You mentioned that just before Mum died, she said something about a home…?" He waited whilst it was clear Kerry was trying to remember.

"'*My home*' so that's what she said, - I think you mentioned she was watching TV at the time when she said it, the morning before she passed away, about lunchtime I seem to remember you mentioning it. Do you know what it was she may have been watching? Oh, yes I'll hold, yes I appreciate you are busy, but it really will help me understand something she left behind for me or at least I hope it will."

He turned to Sally. "Kerry didn't actually hear mum and wasn't in the room herself at the time but the nurse who was with mum is on duty so she's going to ask her."

"But I'm confused James, what are you trying to find out?" Sally looked at him, but his attention switched back to the phone. His face changed to one of incredulity. Open mouthed he listened to the woman on the other end.

"And you're absolutely sure?" He asked. "Thank you, that's really helpful and I appreciate it. Let Kerry know that I appreciate her help as well. Yes, goodbye." He ended the call and sat down deep in thought. Looking back up at Sally as she sat next to him, he actually smiled.

"I think mum got closure after all. Sarah was the one who was with her when she had an odd lucid moment. She didn't say or mean she was in a home i.e., the Nursing Home she was in. The TV programme was the national news and Sarah can remember it showed a cottage and the news that a missing girl's body had been found in Lincolnshire. She must have seen 'Wolds View' cottage on the TV, recognised it and realised they'd found Jenny! She died shortly after that being shown. She wasn't saying she was 'in a home', she was trying to say she'd seen *her old home* on the TV."

They both sat in silence as this sunk in.

A feeling came over him and a resolve took form in his mind. He turned to Sally. "Bear with me in this. Come with me, it's still light." With that he led her down to his car and they drove off in silence. Stopping off at the local garage he picked up some flowers for the graveside and Sally nodded in approval. Her mind was still reeling, none of her cases had ever been this strange she thought as they

A Ghostly Diversion

drove along the small country lanes towards Grasceby.

However, as they approached the Church, a feeling came over James and he drove past it as Sally looked at him oddly, then realised where he was heading.

They pulled up onto the grass verge outside 'Wolds View' cottage and James got out. Sally remained in the car, perplexed and unsure whether to follow.

Walking over and onto the old concrete slab path James stood and looked up at Jenny's window but there was nothing there.

He hesitated and decided he was being silly and turned to go when…

…something caught his eye and he slowly turned back to the cottage…

…looking fresh, lived in with curtains in the windows, Jack, Jenny and Barbara stood smiling at him, reunited at last in death as they couldn't be in life. They looked at him and nodded, waved and began to fade away as they seemed to be hugging each other just as the cottage itself returned to normal.

Sally had been looking away but as she looked back, she noticed James begin to cry but at the same time smile and give a brief wave to someone. She looked at the cottage and for a fleeting moment she thought she could see three figures standing there, but in a blink, they were gone, and a chill rippled down her spine.

James walked back to the car and got in, turned to her and wiped the tears from his eyes.

A Ghostly Diversion

"The circle is complete; they're reunited and at peace at last. Now we know why I was the one Jenny appeared to."

James let his gaze drift off into the distance then back to 'Wolds View'.

"I was family…the brother she would never know in life but found in death and all because of a simple diversion, *a ghostly diversion.*"

He started the car and turned it round, headed back to Grasceby Church. They parked up and walked over and stood next to the graves as James placed the flowers at what he now knew was his family plot.

A whispered voice in his ear brought a tear again to his eyes.

"*Thank you, James.*" said Jenny.

He placed his arm around Sally's waist and together they headed down the church path towards the car knowing that the family was now reunited, and Jenny was at peace at last…

Epilogue

Towards the back of the graveyard a well-dressed, middle-aged gentleman wearing a top hat watched James and Sally leave. He nodded to himself in approval and turned as Jenny appeared next to him and smiled…

"I believe you may well be right my dear. He could very well be the one to help me. Thank you, Jenny. Perhaps at last I may finally find out what became of my nephew and if Annie and he were indeed murdered…"

Authors Note

Although the story is a work of fiction, I wanted to set it in my home county which I feel gets short shrift from authors at times. Reference is made to several towns, villages, and Lincoln itself and they are real places to try to add a little authenticity to the setting. The village of Grasceby, however, is purely fictional as I wanted plenty of leeway to explore the surrounding countryside without compromising any real setting.

The story itself is loosely based on a real incident that occurred to the author when the A158 which leads from Lincoln to Skegness (or the other way round if you live in Skegness!) was undergoing what seemed like quite extensive road works. Caught in the road works I did indeed take a diversion of my own making, along the back roads.

Now you have to remember this was when we still used actual physical road maps, usually large-scale ones and none of these fancy mapping apps on your smart phone or with the car Sat Nav! It was whilst going along this makeshift diversion that several miles along this journey I happened upon a derelict cottage which caught my eye.

It was in good condition, and it struck me it would make a fine property for someone to renovate. Shortly after passing it a thought occurred to me about what my reaction would have been if I'd seen 'a ghostly lady' at one of the windows and a little chill ran down my spine. I carried on driving even though I hadn't seen anything like a ghost and put it out of my thoughts.

A Ghostly Diversion

That is until a few nights later, for some reason, my overactive imagination and thoughts turned back to the cottage and the idea began to develop about a story involving a ghostly girl at the window. Lorraine found that pretty spooky and the rest is history as I developed the idea into a story, but it has to be confessed it took another nine years for the full story to come together. Sometimes these things need a little time to fall into place. As for the route of the 'diversion', that has been mixed up with various turns and bends so as to cause confusion if anyone tries to follow the route in the story.

As for the cottage, who knows if there really is a ghostly lady…

Newsletter

If you enjoy the exploits of James Hansone as he unravels the many ghostly goings on, in and around the sleepy village of Grasceby Lincolnshire, then why not sign up to the newsletter to keep up to date with upcoming novels.

Those signing up will receive a *free* mini novel: "Lord Shabernackles of Grasceby Manor".

So, if you want to know more about the James Hansone Ghost Mysteries or other novels from Astrospace Fiction, such as how to purchase them and where, or when the next book in the series will be released, then simply sign up and you'll be the first to informed. There will also be a possible competition or a give-away so worth subscribing to see what may be on offer soon. Note your information will not be passed on to third parties.

Just head on over to the following link where you can enter your email to be added to the newsletter list.

Note I will not share your email with anybody, and it is only for keeping up to date with Astrospace Fiction books and the James Hansone Ghost Mystery novels.

https://mailchi.mp/1c69765ddf7a/jameshansonegm-signup

Best wishes and see you soon: Paul

The James Hansone Ghost Mysteries

It all started with a simple unplanned diversion, *'A Ghostly Diversion'*.

James Hansone is a computer and IT specialist and a complete sceptic when it came to all things paranormal. Until *that* diversion.

It changes everything once he becomes intrigued with a ghostly face at a broken window of a rundown cottage, deep in the Lincolnshire countryside. Little did he know that he would go on to uncover the mystery of a missing girl that would change his life forever.

Now with four sequels, James Hansone unwittingly becomes a ghost hunter roped in to explore further mysteries with more books planned in the series.

> A Ghostly Diversion
> Secrets of Grasceby Manor
> Return to De Grasceby Manor
> James and the Air of Tragedy
> The Haunting of Grasceby Rectory

All available as kindle, print on demand and Kindle Unlimited from Amazon.

Check out Paul's Amazon author page:
https://www.amazon.co.uk/Paul-L.-Money/e/B003VNGE1M

A Ghostly Diversion

The Fragility of Existence
A Sci-Fi/Apocalyptic tale

The extermination of our species was probably inevitable when you look back with hindsight. Every advanced civilisation has almost always wiped out the resident less advanced occupants whenever they came into contact.

So it was the same for us, Homo Sapiens.
But it wasn't supposed to have happened.
We were not to know that though.
Perhaps that is a good thing.
For the Universe...

Matt and Simone stared out at the devastation and knew it could only mean one thing... Humanity was about to become extinct.
Could they escape the fate they had seen befall others in their small village of 'Woldsfield'?
They were not going to wait around to find out...

Available on Amazon as Kindle, POD and Kindle Unlimited.

A Ghostly Diversion

The *last* Voyage of the StarVista 4

A Voyage of a lifetime.
2700 passengers and crew.
The diary of an eight year old passenger.
Stunning encounters with fabulous interstellar destinations.

The mysterious gas giant planet Tianca in the hardly explored Cantrara system.
A 100 year mystery in the making…
and an old foe re-emerging from exile

Follow the adventures of young Cherice Richmond, the youngest person allowed to undertake an eight month star cruise on board the luxury star cruiser StarVista 4, with her parents, Carl and Natalie, the honourable newly appointed Earth Ambassadors to the Ziancan homeworld.

Little do they know that they will never return…

Available on Amazon as Kindle, POD and Kindle Unlimited.
Book 1 of a trilogy with Book 2: 'The Fate of the StarVista 4' coming soon.

About the Author

Paul L Money is an astronomy broadcaster, writer, public speaker and publisher. He is also the Reviews Editor for the BBC Sky at Night magazine and for eight years until 2013 he was one of three Astronomers on the Omega Holidays Northern Lights Flights. He is married to Lorraine whose hobby/interest is genealogy and family history.

Paul wrote and published the popular annual night sky guide to the year's best night sky events, 'Nightscenes' until it finished in 2021 and also the 'Nightscenes Guide to Simple Astrophotography' with the 2nd edition of the latter almost ready. The latter will be available from Amazon.co.uk when published.

As an astronomer Paul has been giving talks across the UK for thirty years and was awarded the Eric Zuker award for services to astronomy in 2002 by the Federation of Astronomical Societies. In October 2012 he was awarded the 'Sir Arthur Clarke Lifetime Achievement Award, 2012' for his 'tireless promotion of astronomy and space to the public'.

His first novels were ghost stories: 'A Ghostly Diversion' followed by the sequel, 'Secrets of Grasceby Manor', then 'Return to De Grasceby Manor' followed in 2019 with 'James and the Air of

Tragedy' in 2020 and late August 2022, 'The Haunting of Grasceby Rectory' with more planned in the series.

A first foray into the realms of Science Fiction saw the publication of a shorter novel, 'The Fragility of Existence' in early 2019, a version of the 'end of the world' stories that seem popular. 'Fragility of Survival' is coming soon as a standalone follow-on novel with 2 more in the 'Fragility' series also in development.

'The Last Voyage of the StarVista 4' is the first novel to take place in the Galactic Arm Association (GAA) Universe and was published in November 2021. The sequel, 'The Fate of the StarVista 4' is expected mid 2023 followed by 'The Legacy of the StarVista 4'.

Another novel almost ready: 'This New Horizon' will also have two sequels but whose story will eventually link up with the saga begun with 'The Last Voyage of the StarVista 4'.

More info can be found at his Astrospace web site:
Astrospace/ Astrospace publications
http://www.astrospace.co.uk

April 2023

Printed in Great Britain
by Amazon